社交
英文書信

Janusz Buda
長野格 　著
城戶保男

羅慧娟 　譯

三民書局

前　言

　　企業界對一般書信往來（訂單、出貨說明等），因書寫機會多，較為熟悉；但對於社交書信，特別是弔唁信等，書寫的機會並不多，往往令人不知如何下筆。況且這些時候多屬突發狀況，筆者等人服務於企業界時，也曾有過因突發的需要，而慌忙地四處翻尋例文的經驗。

　　大約去年春末，我們接受出版社的委託，希望能出版一本因應時代潮流，符合上述社交書信需求的書。

　　我們隨即分工，由 Buda 根據實例寫作英文範例，再由長野和城戶，添加翻譯及語句注釋。為了避免限於個人狹隘的觀點，在 Buda 暑假回到英國時，我們藉由網路上的不斷往返討論，也讓本書的內容更為全面化。因為這樣的經驗，我們在本書中也加入了一些以電子郵件替代傳統書信的例子。

　　本書所採用的範例幾乎全是根據實際情形使用過的書信，絕非憑空杜撰的。這些文章都經筆者三人慎重地推敲考量下，集結而成本書。

　　然而，因本書全以實例為基礎所編寫而成，難免在某些特殊狀況下有缺乏一般性之虞。期望讀者遇到此情況時，以本書的範例作為參考，寫成適合自己的書信。大體而言，書中之範例，大部分只需要經過些許修改，即可直接使用，盼讀者能多方加以活用。

　　最後，對現已從研究社退休，赴大學任教之本書前任編輯久田正晴先生的多方激勵及建言，和接任其工作的黑岩佳代子小姐，在此致上衷心的謝意。

1997 年 7 月

著者謹誌

社交英文書信

目　次

序章

商業書信的格式

就商業書信的格式而言，習慣上有數種架構。以下舉四種一般較為常見的例子，就其構成要素加以說明。此外，標點符號的使用，一般也都有固定的格式，在此與例文一起加以說明。

一、構成要素

商業書信大體上，呈現如第 3 頁附圖般的形式，以下就其各部分構成要素，一一作說明。以下的說明中 ①、②……等號碼，與第 3 頁附圖的書信範例中之 ①、②……等號碼相對應。

①書信信頭 (Letterhead)

一般由發信者的公司名稱、地址、電話號碼、商務電報號碼、傳真號碼等所組成，通常各公司行號會直接印刷於信紙上，無須個別書寫或打字。

②發信日期欄 (Date Line)

最普遍的書寫方式如下：

美式：April 2, 2001

英式：2nd April, 2001

今後，受電子郵件日益普遍的影響，可能更為簡化的書寫方式將日趨增加，不過如 4–2–01 般，只有數字的寫法，應儘可能地避免，因為在美國會被解釋為 4 月 2 日，在英國卻會被認為是 2 月 4 日。

③信中附加收信者住址 (Inside Address)

信紙上列入與信封上相同的收信者姓名、住址。這是為了雙方便於整理文件，或第三者收到此信副本時，可憑此確認發信者。此項，日後也可能因電子郵件的普及化而改變。

④開頭稱謂語 (Salutation)

相當於中文書信中「稱謂」及「提稱語」的部分。現在，即使在公司行號中，發信給特定個人的情形亦相當普遍，故以使用 Dear Mr. 的方式最為常見。當然，Mr. 的稱謂，也因對象的不同而可更替為 Mrs./ Miss./ Ms./ Dr. 等。若非針對特定的個人，而以公司行號為發信對象時，則不使用 Mr. 等稱謂，而改用 Dear Sirs 或 Ladies and Gentlemen 等的開頭稱謂語。在美國，過去一直沿用 Gentlemen，現在已幾乎不復見。

發信給特定個人的情況通常使用 Dear Mr. Smith 或 Dear John 二種形式。前者附帶敬稱 (Mr.) 的情形，一般後面只寫姓。發信給非常熟稔或親近的對象，直接稱呼名字的情形，則決不附加敬稱。因此，有如 Dear Mr John 或 Dear Miss Joan 等，皆為錯誤的用法。此外，須注意開頭稱謂語

中不以全名稱呼。也就是，通常不寫作 Dear Mr. John B. Smith 或 Dear Joan Foster 等。

開頭稱謂語後面加標點符號時（Mixed Punctuation 及 Closed Punctuation 的情況下），美式用法使用冒號，英式用法則使用逗點。但若為私人信件時，美式用法中也使用逗點。

⑤本文 (Body of the Letter)

本書中的每一篇書信，均附有詳細的中譯及語句注釋，故不在此多作說明。在書寫格式上，採用一般常見的「全文靠左」(Block Letter) 格式。標點符號的使用，與書寫一般英文書信方式相同。

⑥結尾敬辭 (Complimentary Close)

相當於中文書信中的「謹上」、「敬上」等的結尾部分。英式用法中對初次往來的對象，開頭稱謂語使用 Dear Sir 或 Dear Sirs 等敬稱時，結尾敬

---

① **IMAI INTERNATIONAL**
Parkside Building 9F, Aoyama 1−1−1, Minato-ku, Tokyo 107
Tel: 03 (3320) 6255　Fax: 03 (3320) 6250

② August 20, 2000

③ Mr. Louis E. Potter
Chief Executive Officer
Mariner Electronic Industries
444 East William Street
Ann Arbor, MI 48104
U. S. A.

④ Dear Mr. Potter:

⑤ May I congratulate you on your promotion to the post of Chief Executive Officer of Mariner Electronic Industries.

In the five years we have been doing business together, I have become closely acquainted with your exceptional managerial talents, and I know that the future of Mariner is in capable hands.

I am supremely confident that the solid business ties that link our two companies will continue to grow and develop, and that we can work together to forge an unbeatable alliance.

I look forward to meeting you at next month's Electronics Expo in Boston.

⑥ Yours sincerely,

⑦ *Taro Yamada*
Taro Yamada
Vice President

⑧ TY:fn

Modified Block Letter 的範例（參照構成要素 ①〜⑧）

辭通常使用 Yours faithfully。對一般已熟稔的對象，則大多使用 Yours sincerely。美式用法中則多使用 Sincerely 或 Sincerely yours。然而，有時也因對象的不同使用如下的敬辭。

Very truly yours; Yours truly; Cordially yours; Cordially; Very sincerely yours; Very cordially yours

⑦署名部分 (Signature Block)

結尾敬辭下，空四行左右，打字附上發信人姓名。然後，在空下的部分，親筆簽上姓名。過去習慣在結尾敬辭的下面，以大寫打上發函者的公司名稱，近來則普遍省略。

⑧其他要素 (Other Notations)

(i)發信相關人的姓名縮寫 (Identification Marks)

在過去，如下附上發函者和打字者的姓名開頭縮寫的方式，曾經相當普遍。

TY: fn（發函者為 Taro Yamada，打字者為 Frances Newman）。

然近來，通常只標示打字員姓名開頭字母的縮寫。

打字員的姓名縮寫雖也可使用英文字母大寫，不過一般以小寫字母較多。再者，近來的信件往往不經由打字員，而由發函者親自打字，在此情況下，則不須附加此要項。

(ii)隨函附加物件的註明 (Enclosure Notation)

隨函附加任何物件時，務必在信函的左下角，如下所示般地，加以註明。此作法主要是請收件人查收附加物件，同時也有提醒寄件人不忘記封入欲寄物件之效。寫法大體上如下所示。

Enclosure（僅附加 1 物件時）

Enclosures（附加 2 物件以上時）

也有如下所示，詳細標明所附物件的名稱。

Enclosures : 1. Catalog, 2 copies

　　　　　　2. Order Form, 2 Copies

(iii)副本抄送對象 (CC Notation)

副本抄送第三者的情形，其書寫方式如下。

cc: Mr. J. W. Smith

　　Ms. Janet B. Gilbert

cc 原為 carbon copy（複寫紙複印）的縮寫。不過，此種夾複寫紙於打字機上，製作副本的方式，已極為罕見，現在多以影印機直接作成影

本，因此有時以 pc（photo copy 的縮寫），或單以 c 表示。

不過，現在電子郵件上一般也使用 CC 的用法。此處，當然不是指 carbon copy，而是 courtesy copy。此要項可以字母大寫或小寫表示。

(iv)附註 (Postscript)

本文後加附註時，以 P.S. 或 PS. 表示，然後寫上欲註明的事項，之後簽上發函者的姓名縮寫即可。

二、書寫格式 (Style)

❶Block Letter（請參照第 7 頁）

為書寫時全文各行向左端靠齊的一種格式，可省去段落起始縮排 (Indent) 的麻煩。不過，因令人有偷工減料的感覺，對於初次接觸的對象，或有必要相當注意禮儀的情況時，不宜採用。一般公司內部的聯絡，或對公司以外熟稔的對象，在目前普遍使用此一全文靠左的格式。然因有各段落之間難以辨識的缺點，一般在各段落之間空一行，便於閱讀。

❷Modified Block Letter（請參照第 8 頁）

與上述的 Block Letter 幾乎完全相同，只是將發信日期和最後的署名部分往右端靠齊。Block Letter 因全文靠左因而重心偏左，感覺不太平衡，此修正過的 Modified Block Letter，在架構上令人感覺較為平衡。不過，因本文的每一行全向左靠，故務必在段落之間空一行，以易於辨識。

❸ Modified Semi-block Letter（請參照第 9 頁）

將上述的 Modified Block Letter 更加以延伸，使每一段落開始首行內縮，為四種架構中，最為保守的格式，在鍵盤操作上雖有若干不便，卻可說是禮貌最為周到的一種格式。公司內部的聯繫等，以不麻煩的 Block Form 即可，然對於初次往來的對象或須注意到禮儀時，使用此格式應較為適切。

❹ Simplified Letter（請參照第 10 頁）

與 Block Letter 同樣，將全文各行往左端靠齊，不過省掉開頭稱謂語和結尾敬辭二部分。隨著傳真機以及電子郵件等尖端通訊媒體的廣泛使用，一般認為，使用此簡化格式的例子也將日益增多。不過，務必留意不要在須注意到禮儀的場合，使用此格式。

三、標點句讀法

標點句讀法一般有下列三種。

① Open Punctuation

本文以外的各行末尾完全不加標點符號的方式。不過，像 Co. 等的縮寫

省略符號，恰巧置於行末時，仍應保留。

Simplified Letter 中一定使用此種標點符號方式，此外，Block Letter 中也經常使用。

② Mixed Punctuation

本文之外的構成要素之中，於開頭稱謂語和最後的結尾敬辭二部分加標點，其他部分則採不加標點的一種方式。至於開頭稱謂語後的標點，美式用法為冒號，英式用法則為逗點。不過，若是私人的書信，美式用法中也使用逗點。

Mixed Punctuation 現在傾向於不使用在 Simplified Letter 或 Block Letter 中。

③ Closed Punctuation

乃於本文之外的各構成要素的行末，全部附加標點符號的方式，然因太過煩雜，現在幾乎已不為人採用。其內容如下。

(i)發信日期行末加句點。

(ii)收信人住址欄中，最後一行以外的每一行末皆加逗點，最後一行則加句點。

(iii)開頭稱謂語後，美式用法加冒號，美式用法加逗點。私人信件中美式用法也使用逗點。

(iv)結尾敬辭後加逗點。

(v)簽名欄中，最後一行之外的每一行末加逗點，最後一行則加句點。

　　由下頁起依序為 4 種格式的範例 ❶～❹。至於標點句讀法，❶～❸為 mixed punctuation，❹則為 open punctuation。

SHIRAI TRADING

4–3–1 Nishikanda, Chiyoda-ku, Tokyo, 101 JAPAN

Tel: 03–5689–3201
Fax: 03–5689–3202
Email: shiri@net.co.jp

July 18, 2001

Mr. Frederick T. Jarvis
Executive Vice President
Hammond Corporation
405 Johns Blvd.
Ypsilanti, MI 481907
U. S. A.

Dear Mr. Jarvis:

It was with great pleasure that I read in this morning's newspaper that you had received the Thomas F. Edelstein Award in recognition of your many contributions to the field of international commerce.

I can think of no more worthy recipient of this prestigious award, and feel certain that the selecting committee has made an excellent choice.

This award brings honor not only to your good self, but to the entire industry of which you are such an illustrious representative.

Please accept my warmest congratulations, and those of everyone here at Shirai Trading.

Yours sincerely,

Joji Ueda

Joji Ueda, Vice President

IMAI INTERNATIONAL

Parkside Building 9F, Aoyama 1−1−1, Minato-ku, Tokyo 107

Tel: 03 (3320) 6255   Fax: 03 (3320) 6250

August 20, 2001

Mr. Louis E. Potter
Chief Executive Officer
Mariner Electronic Industries
444 East William Street
Ann Arbor, MI 48104
U. S. A.

Dear Mr. Potter:

May I congratulate you on your promotion to the post of Chief Executive Officer of Mariner Electronic Industries.

In the five years we have been doing business together, I have become closely acquainted with your exceptional managerial talents, and I know that the future of Mariner is in capable hands.

I am supremely confident that the solid business ties that link our two companies will continue to grow and develop, and that we can work together to forge an unbeatable alliance.

I look forward to meeting you at next month's Electronics Expo in Boston.

Yours sincerely,

Taro Yamada

Taro Yamada

TY:fn

Grange House
20, Malvern Lane
Riverbridge RA5 7JH
Telephone: 01345 568223
Fax: 01345 568225

CHALMERS & OWEN

PUBLISHERS

18th March, 2001

Williams Publishing PLC
Walton Street
Oxford OX2 6DP
England

Dear Sirs,

It is with deep regret that we have to announce the death, on March 17, of Cecily Monroe, the director of our advertising department.

It was Cecily's express wish that she be given a private funeral, and that the announcement of her death be not made until after the funeral had taken place.

Desmond Rogers has agreed to take over Cecily's department until a permanent replacement can be found, and all messages of condolence should be addressed to him.

Yours faithfully,

Arthur M. Price

Arthur M. Price
Vice President

AMP:ft

AEROGLOBE COURIERS

Across Five Continents

2200 Eastern Boulevard	8-3, Fujimidai 2 chome
Watsonville CA 95076	Shizuoka City 422
408−760−2020	054−524−3385

March 5, 2001

Mr. Chor Sun Kee, Manager
Personnel Department
Aeroglobe Couriers Ltd.
12−1 Honcho 2−chome
Chiyoda-ku, Tokyo 101

REQUEST FOR RECONSIDERATION OF MY TRANSFER

I was deeply disturbed to learn that I am due to be transferred to the Maebashi Branch in April.

The announcement of the transfer came as a complete surprise. As you know, I have worked in the Shizuoka Branch for over six years, and have been very happy here.

I am not sure upon what basis the transfer decision was taken, or why I was not consulted in the matter.

I ask you to reconsider this decision. If my services are no longer required here in Shizuoka, I am prepared to submit my resignation.

Saburo Yamada

Saburo Yamada
Sales Promotion, Shizuoka Branch

cc: Mr. Shiro Tanaka, Promotion Manager

1

慶唁

由早報上得知業界的翹楚，且與自己公司有客戶往來關係的知名人士，獲頒非常榮譽獎項之消息，立即提筆道賀的書信。

Dear Mr. Jarvis,

It was with great pleasure that I read in this morning's newspaper that you had received the Thomas F. Edelstein Award **in recognition of** your many contributions to the field of international commerce.

I can think of no more worthy recipient of this **prestigious award**, and feel certain that the selecting committee has made an excellent choice.

This award brings honor not only to **your good self**, but to the entire industry of which you are **such an illustrious representative**.

Please accept **my warmest congratulations**, and those of everyone here at Swanson Trading Incorporated.

Yours sincerely,

賈維斯先生台鑒：

　　今晨於報上欣聞閣下獲頒愛德爾斯丁獎 (Thomas F. Edelstein Award)，肯定您對於國際貿易領域的諸多貢獻。

　　如此深具獲獎資格者，除閣下外，實不作他人之想。我並深信此獎的遴選委員會，著實作了最明智的選擇。

　　此次獲獎，不僅為閣下帶來殊榮，整個業界更因有閣下如此傑出的代表，而同感榮耀。

　　本人謹代表史汪森貿易公司全體同仁，衷心獻上最真誠的祝福。

　　　　　　　　　　　　　　　　　　　　　　　　　　　　謹上

【語句注釋】◆ **in recognition of ～**　「肯定，認可」，也具「表揚」之意。(= as a recognition of)　◆ **prestigious award**　「極具聲望的獎賞」。prestigious 含有「高級的，一流的」之意，有時也指 the most prestigious brand「最高級的名牌」等。◆ **your good self**　「閣下，您」。在此指得獎者，在舊式商業書信中，以複數形 your good selves 指「貴公司」。　◆ **such an illustrious representative**　「極為傑出的代表」。such 放在單一的名詞之前時，用以強調該名詞。You are such a liar.（你是個大騙子）。illustrious「傑出的；著名的」。◆ **my warmest congratulations**　「我最衷心的祝福」。warm 指話語等，「溫暖，誠心，真誠的」之意，經常使用於祝福時的形容詞，意同 hearty, sincere 等。此外，congratulations 為「賀辭」之意，必須用複數。

【注意】若由得獎者本人主動告知獲頒獎項一事，通常總感覺有些彆扭。當從報紙上得知消息，若能在本人告知之前，儘早為文道賀的話，想必得獎者將從祝福的賀辭中，感受到更多的喜悅。

祝賀昇職的書信中，主要針對欲致賀的當事人，其才能如何地適合昇任新職，以及藉由此昇職，確信今後雙方公司之間關係，將益發緊密等二點，撰寫賀辭。

Dear Mr. Potter,

May I congratulate you on your promotion to the post of Chief Executive Officer of Mariner Electronics.

In the five years we have been doing business together, I have become closely acquainted with your exceptional managerial talents, and I know that the future of Mariner is in capable hands.

I am supremely confident that the solid business ties that link our two companies will continue to grow and develop, and that we can work together to forge an unbeatable alliance.

I look forward to meeting you at next month's Electronics Expo in Boston.

Yours sincerely,

波特先生台鑒：

　　謹以此信，恭祝閣下昇任瑪麗娜電器公司之最高經營負責人。
　　近 5 年來，榮幸與閣下共事，已非常熟悉閣下實為深具卓越經營管理才能之負責人，並深知瑪麗娜的未來，掌握在閣下有能之手中。
　　敝人深信貴公司與敝公司間堅實的商業合作關係，必將持續地成長與發展。更確信我們將進而共同偕力地建立堅不可摧的合作關係。
　　期待下個月於波士頓的電器博覽會上，與閣下會面。

謹上

【語句注釋】◆ become closely acquainted with ～　「熟知～，精通～」。◆ your exceptional managerial talents 「閣下之卓越經營手腕、才能」。exceptional 在這裏用作「極為卓越，無與倫比的」之意。talents 指「才能」。◆ be in capable hands 「掌握在有能者之手中」。in hand 有「支配，管理」之意。◆ I am supremely confident that 「堅信，深信」。形容詞 supreme，通常用於「最高的，至高的」之意，在此 supremely 為副詞，表「非常地，極度地」之意。◆ solid business ties 「堅實的商業關係」。tie 本指「繩子，繩索，領帶」等，在此 business ties 使用複數形時，意指「牽繫，聯繫，關係」。◆ to forge an unbeatable alliance 「創造出堅實的合作關係」。forge 本為「鑄造、鍛造（劍等）」之意。unbeatable 為「無敵的」。alliance 為「同盟，合作」。

1–3 生日的祝賀辭

在陳述祝賀之意的同時，告知附上小禮物以表心意。

Dear Mr. Franklin,

Many congratulations on your birthday, and best wishes for many years to come.

I am sending you a small gift which I hope will remind you of your visit to our Aomori factory last year. I do hope you like it.

Please give my best regards to your wife and family.

Yours sincerely,

1–4 祝賀結婚紀念日

祝賀結婚 50 週年的同時，期望早日再度相會。

Dear Mr. and Mrs. Silverman:

Please accept my heartiest congratulations on the fiftieth anniversary of your marriage.

I sincerely hope that the years to come will bring you much joy and happiness, and that it won't be too long before we have a chance to meet again.

Yours truly,

富蘭克林先生台鑒：

　　生日快樂。並衷心祝福來年之長壽康泰。
　　隨信附上一份小禮，希望看見它會令您想起去年閣下來訪敝公司青森工廠之情景。希望您會喜歡。
　　請代吾人向夫人及家人轉達問候之意。

謹上

席佛蒙先生、夫人同鑒：

　　在此為閣下之 50 週年結婚紀念日，獻上最真誠的祝福。
　　吾人由衷祈望閣下往後的日子充滿喜悅與幸福，並且期盼不久的將來，能有機會再相見。

謹上

此信內容傳達了獲知友人退休，希望其今後能過得健康、幸福的生活等祝福的話語以及感謝工作上的多方協助，並致贈作為紀念的禮物等。

Dear Mr. Yarrow,

Many thanks for your letter of October 15, informing me of your retirement from T & A Publishing.

In addition to wishing you many years of health and happiness, I should like to take this opportunity to thank you for all the help and support you gave Tom Smith, Amy Tang, Jerry Thomas, Nicholas Moyer, and many other of our young artists in their efforts to establish themselves in the United States market.

All of us will forever remain deeply indebted to you, and as a token of our appreciation we are sending you a small commemorative plaque engraved with our signatures.

Yours very sincerely,

耶羅先生台鑒：

　　十分謝謝您 10 月 15 日的來信，告知已從 T & A 出版社退休一事。

　　首先祈祝閣下身體健康與幸福，並藉此機會向閣下致上深忱的感謝。感激閣下多方提拔湯姆・史密斯、湯艾美、傑瑞・湯瑪士、尼古拉・摩耶，以及其他許多敝公司旗下之年輕藝術家，打入美國市場，並給予諸多協助。

　　敝公司全體同仁將永遠感懷閣下之恩澤。在此致上刻有全體同仁署名之紀念匾額，作為表達我們感謝之意的象徵。

謹呈

【語句注釋】◆ I should like to ～　「想要～，欲～」。也可使用 I would like to ～。在美國 would 比 should 更常用。◆ establish themselves　「（在某範疇）立身、奠定地位」。◆ indebted to ～　「受～之恩，感激」。remain indebted to ～「永遠感懷某人之恩澤」。◆ commemorative plaque　「紀念匾額」。plaque「飾板，匾額，裝飾用的額板」。◆ engraved with signatures　「刻上署名」。

收到先前有生意往來的友人，找到新工作的通知（範例 8-9）後，祝賀再就職的同時，並期望再相會的回信。

Dear Mr. Bailey,

Please let me express my **heartiest congratulations on** your new position with Ta-ming Electrical Motors. The company is fortunate indeed to have acquired such a talented and experienced businessman as yourself, and I am sure that, under your **capable direction**, the export department will be able to expand into many attractive overseas markets.

I was delighted to hear that there is a possibility that you might come to **the States** next year. Please do try to **fit a visit** to the South **into your schedule**, and let me know as soon as possible when you'll be coming.

I'm looking forward to seeing you again **before too long**.

Yours sincerely,

貝利先生台鑒：

　　衷心地祝賀您就任大明電動馬達公司之新職。該公司能招攬像您如此有才能，且深具豐富商務經驗的人才，實值慶幸。吾人更相信，在您強而有力的領導下，旗下的外銷部門必能拓展到許多眾所矚目的海外市場。

　　很高興獲知您極有可能在明年來訪美國。若果真成行，請務必將造訪南部排入您預定的行程，並及早告知我您將來訪。

　　期待在不久的將來，就能與您再見面。

　　　　　　　　　　　　　　　　　　　　　　　　　　　　　　謹上

　　祝賀筆友的女兒弄瓦之喜，並提及家族能就近照顧極令人羨慕的問候信。

Dear Mr. Evanson,

Please let me congratulate you on becoming a grandfather!

You and your wife must be very proud indeed of your new granddaughter.

Your **son-in-law** showed me some photographs of her when he was in Tokyo last week, and she looks a truly pretty and delightful little girl.

In many ways I envy you living so near to your daughter and her family. My own children live far away from us–my son Taro in Australia, and my daughter Sachiko in Singapore. We **keep in touch by phone and letter**, but my wife and I often **wish they were a little nearer to us**.

Please give my best regards to Mrs. Evanson. I do hope she is feeling a little better these days.

Yours sincerely,

艾文森先生台鑒：

　　恭禧您當了外祖父！

　　您和尊夫人，想必相當以剛誕生的外孫女為榮。

　　上個禮拜，令千金的夫婿來東京時，讓我們看了令孫女的照片，她看起來真是個漂亮可愛的小嬰孩。

　　在許多方面，我真羨慕您與令千金及其家人住得如此鄰近。我的孩子與我們相隔遙遠——兒子太郎在澳洲，女兒幸子住在新加坡。雖然我們經常以電話或寫信聯絡，但我和內人總希望他們能夠住得靠近些。

　　請代我向令夫人傳達最誠摯的問候，並衷心盼望近來她的身體較為安好。

　　　　　　　　　　　　　　　　　　　　　　　　　　　　謹上

【語句注釋】◆ Please let me congratulate you on becoming a grandfather!「恭禧您當了外祖父！」亦可說 Congratulations on (your) becoming a grandfather. 注意介系詞為 on。◆ son-in-law 「女婿」。father-in-law「丈人」。brother-in-law「姐夫或妹婿」。in-law 表示姻親的關係。◆ keep in touch 「保持聯繫」。◆ by phone and letter 「藉由電話和書信」。通常在表示手段的 by 之後，不加冠詞。如 by ship, by bicycle, by fax 等。◆ I wish they were a little nearer to us. 「真希望他們住得靠近些。」此句用過去式表示與現在事實相反的假設。實際上因不住在附近，而感到遺憾。

　　回覆對方寄來的聖誕卡片，同時回顧過去的一年，並祈祝新的一年生意興隆，以及告知明年 3 月或許有機會見面的一封致謝信。

Dear Mr. Foster:

Thank you so much for your beautiful Christmas card.

The last year certainly presented plenty of business problems to us, however, I feel that we **got through them quite well**. I would hope that this year would be prosperous and trouble-free for all of us, but the reality is that the American slang expression **"nothing comes easy" is all too true**. I wish you and your family a happy and prosperous new year.

I have spoken to Mr. Lin and am tentatively planning to be in the Far East the first week in March. I will certainly look forward to seeing you if **your schedule calls for you to be in Taipei**.

Kindest personal regards,

福斯特先生台鑒：

　　非常感謝您寄來如此精美的聖誕卡片。
　　過去的一年，我們的確遭逢許多業務上的困難，不過我想我們已順利地度過了重重的難關。希望今年我們都將有個豐收平順的一年。然而現實，卻有如美國俗諺說的「事事不易」啊！希望閣下和家人有個快樂富足的新年。
　　我與林先生洽談過，暫定 3 月的第一個禮拜前往遠東地區。若您有前往臺北的行程計畫的話，我非常期待能與您相會。

　　　　　　　　　　　　　　　　　　　　　　　　　　謹上

【語句注釋】◆ got through them quite well 「順利地度過」。them 在此指 problems。◆ "nothing comes easy" is all too true 「『事事不易』這句話實在太貼切」。all too ～ 指「那麼的，極其地」，也就是口語中 very very 的意思。◆ your schedule calls for you to be in Taipei 「閣下的行程使您必須到臺北」。在此 call for 與 require 同。◆ Kindest personal regards 「衷心地致上個人的問候」。

原本預定前往訪問，不巧對方因病住院，而未能相見。此信除了告知自己的訪問外，並致上慰問之意。

Dear Mr. Hamilton,

I was disappointed not to be able to meet you on my business trip to New Zealand last week, and saddened to hear that you were in hospital.

Your secretary told me that you had not been feeling very well recently, and had experienced a mild heart attack on the day before I arrived in Dunedin. I do hope you are feeling better now, and are well on the road to recovery.

I am sure that you will be out of hospital in no time at all, and that I'll have an opportunity to see you again on my next visit to New Zealand.

Yours sincerely,

漢米爾頓先生台鑒：

　　很遺憾上星期到紐西蘭出差時未能與您見面，並難過地得知您因病住院的消息。

　　您的祕書告訴我，您近來總覺身體不適，而在我抵達丹尼丁的前一日，您適逢輕度的心臟病發作。我誠摯地希望現在您的身體狀況已經好轉，並順利地復原之中。

　　深信您將很快地即可出院，並在我下回造訪紐西蘭時，有機會能再與您見面。

　　　　　　　　　　　　　　　　　　　　　　　　　　　　謹上

【語句注釋】◆ **on my business trip** 「因公出差旅行時」。在此 on 表示「～時」，與 when I visited on business 大體上語義相同。◆ **be saddened to hear** ～ 「聽到～而難過」。sadden 為「使悲傷，難過」之及物動詞，自身難過時，注意須以被動語態表示。◆ hospital 「住院」。住院的說法，不須加冠詞，不寫作 in the hospital 或 in a hospital。out of hospital 「出院」的說法也相同。◆ **be well on the road to** ～ 「順利地邁向～之，順利地朝向～方向」。在此 well 意指「順利地」。

【注意】撰寫此類帶有遺憾的信函時，須留意千萬不要傷及對方的感情。另外，在表達慰問、同情之意時，別忘了為對方加油、打氣。

收到往來客戶寄來的受災慰問函，向其關懷之意致謝，並報告現狀。

Dear Mr. Nakajima:

Your **concern** about the flooding situation in Holland is very much appreciated by all the members of our company.

At this moment about 250,000 people have been **evacuated** from their homes. The **crisis area** is in the center and southern part of Holland. Therefore it does not affect our company **in a direct way**, and we do not have to be evacuated. At this moment the situation is stable and the water level is sinking slowly. We have **a good hope** that all the people can return to their homes by the end of next week.

At the same time we also would like to express our concern and deep sympathy to all the people in Japan who have lost family, friends and homes during the earthquake in the Kobe area. **Having seen the pictures of this disaster makes us realize** that the problems we have are **of minor importance**. We wish the Japanese people all the strength they need to **overcome** this major disaster.

Thanks again for your concern!

With the very best regards,

中島先生台鑒：

　　非常感激您對荷蘭此地洪水氾濫的情況表示關切，本公司全體同仁謹在此致上謝忱。

　　目前，約 25 萬戶居民被疏散避難。最危險的地區位在荷蘭的中、南部。因此，本公司並未受到直接的影響，故沒有避難的必要。目前受災的情況已平穩下來，水位也緩慢地降低。預計在下個禮拜，所有避難的人應可回到自己的家園。

　　同時，我們也衷心地向在神戶大地震中，喪失了家人、朋友以及家園的日本人們致上同情之意。照片上呈現地震災害的慘狀，令我們了解到自己所面臨的問題實在微不足道。我們祈望所有受災的日本人們有足夠的力量與信心克服度過此次大災害。

　　再度地感謝閣下的關切。

　　　　　　　　　　　　　　　　　　　　　　　　　　　　　謹上

【語句注釋】◆ concern 「關心；擔心」。◆ evacuate 「使避難，使疏散」。注意此動詞為及物動詞，不是「避難」，而是「使避難」之意，故自發性避難時，必須以被動語態的 We were evacuated 表示，而非 We evacuated。名詞為 evacuation。◆ crisis area 「危險地帶，危機四伏的地區」。◆ in a direct way 「直接地」。大致上與 directly 同義。◆ a good hope 「極高的可能性」。◆ Having seen the pictures of this disaster makes us realize～ 「看到災害的照片，使我們體認到 ～」。也就是「看到災害的照片，我們了解 ～」的意思。在英語中，經常使用以無生物為主詞的句子。◆ of minor importance 「不太重要」。not very important 之意。◆ overcome 「克服（困難）」。

通知本公司的廣告部經理於日前逝世，並已舉行私人葬禮的消息。同時通知暫定的職務代理人。

Dear Sirs,

It is **with deep regret** that we have to announce the death, on March 17, of Cecily Monroe, the director of our advertising department.

It was Cecily's **express wish** that she be given a **private funeral**, and that the announcement of her death be not made until after the funeral had taken place.

Desmond Rogers has agreed to **take over** Cecily's department until a **permanent replacement** can be found, and all messages of **condolence** should be addressed to him.

Yours faithfully,

敬啟者：

　　茲以極悲慟的心情通知您本公司之廣告部經理莎西莉·門羅已於3月17日離開人世。

　　並遵照故人之遺囑，直到私人葬禮結束之後，才作正式的死亡通知。

　　戴斯蒙·羅傑已同意暫時替代故人之職務，直至本公司決定正式的後繼人選。故所有弔唁慰問信函，請指名羅傑收付。

謹呈

【語句注釋】◆ with deep regret 「深感哀慟」之意。◆ express wish 「明確的希望」。此處，express 表示「清楚的，明白的」之意。◆ private funeral 「私人葬禮」。◆ take over 「繼任」。◆ permanent replacement 「正式的繼任」。permanent 在此有「長久的；常任的」之意。與 temporary「暫時的，一時的」相對。◆ condolence 「弔唁，慰問」。

【注意】針對此類報喪通知的回函中，應儘量避免詢問死因或大作文章地發抒哀悼之意，應體諒對方的心情，讓此事靜靜沈澱。

得知有生意往來的公司總經理去世的消息，表達哀悼之意的弔唁信。

Dear Mr. Gardiner:

We were deeply saddened to hear of the death of Mr. Simon Warrington, the president of your company.

His contribution to the **furtherance** of trade between our two countries was **immeasurable**, and he will be **sorely** missed by everyone who knew him.

Please accept our sincerest condolences, and convey our deepest sympathy to his family in their **bereavement**.

Yours sincerely,

賈汀納先生台鑒:

　　獲悉貴公司總經理塞蒙‧渥林頓先生去世的消息，在此深表哀慟之意。

　　其為振興兩國之間的貿易所作的貢獻，實在無法計量。所有認識他的人，也將為其深懷哀慟之情。

　　在此由衷地表示哀悼，並請代為向其家人轉達慰問之意。

　　　　　　　　　　　　　　　　　　　　　　　　　　　謹上

【語句注釋】◆ We were deeply saddened 「我們深感哀慟」。sadden 為「使哀慟」及物動詞，We sadden (a person) 則表示「我們使某人哀傷」之意，要表示「我們很悲傷」，務必使用被動語態 We are saddened。◆ furtherance 「促進，助長」。其語義大致與 promotion 相同，不過 furtherance 比較正式。◆ immeasurable 「不可計量的」。measurable「可計量的」。im- 為表示否定的字首。◆ sorely 「很，非常，極」。大致上與 deeply 同義，不過一方面前面已使用過 deeply，另一方面使用 sorely 較為正式。此外，sorely 大多與表示「哀慟」等的字彙連用，故不用於喜事上。◆ bereavement 「死別；喪親之痛」。

【注意】撰寫此類信函時，因英文與中文之間，表現形式上有時迥異，若直譯易造成語意不明。上述的譯文，乃是考量此差異下作成；相反地，將中文譯為英文時也相同。若因疏而失禮，特地致函表示哀悼的心意反而造成反效果。故有必要慎重地選擇適當的用語。

接到有生意往來的埃凡先生的死訊後，在表示哀悼之意的同時，並言及若有需要幫忙之處，請直言告知。

Dear Mr. Jansen:

Your letter informing us of the untimely death of Tom Evans came as a terrible shock.

All of us here at Muraoka Fabrics were stunned by the news, and feel at a loss for words.

Please accept our deepest sympathies, and please let us know if there is any way that we can be of assistance to you at this unfortunate time.

Sincerely yours,

詹森先生台鑒:

　　收到閣下告知湯姆・埃凡先生猝死的信函，深感驚愕。
　　村岡紡織公司的我等全體同仁，皆因此死訊震驚不已，不知該述
何言。
　　在此衷心地致上最深的哀悼之意。同時，若有任何需要我們幫忙
之處，亦請直言告知。

　　　　　　　　　　　　　　　　　　　　　　　　　　　　謹上

【語句注釋】◆ untimely 「意料之外」。本意為「時間未到，過早」，在此為因事故或
其原因而猝死之意。◆ fabrics 「紡織」。◆ be stunned 「驚愕」。stun 為及物動詞，
使驚愕」之意。因此，要表示「我們感到驚愕」時，務必使用被動語態 We are stunned。
◆ feel at a loss for words 「不知該述何言」。feel 亦可以 be 動詞代替。◆ sympathies
弔唁的慰問話語」。sympathy 表示抽象意義的「同情」時，為不可數名詞；不過在此用複
數形表示「弔唁之辭，慰問的話語」之意。

2

邀請函

簡介新產品發表會的同時，延請往來多年的經銷商出席的邀請函。並請求其參與最後的壓軸演出。

Dear Mr. Sanders,

The launch date of our new camping trailer, the "Evergreen", is now set for September 22nd.

In addition to prime-time advertising slots on both radio and TV, and full-page spreads in all the major newspapers, we have reserved the Rainbow Hall in the Hotel Splendide Annexe for what promises to be the most thrilling product launch ever.

As one of our oldest and most successful dealers, we would like to show our appreciation of your contribution to the success of our company by inviting you to take part in the finale of the presentation.

Our Special Promotions Department is still working on the details, but we hope to arrange for one of our Evergreen trailers to be lowered from the ceiling, and for several beauty queens to emerge from the trailer and present bouquets of flowers to our three leading dealers. Camera crews from at least three TV networks will be at the event, and I'm sure it will result in an enormous amount of top-drawer publicity for all of us.

Please let me know if you can come and join us in this thrilling product launch.

Yours sincerely,

桑德斯先生台鑒:

　　本公司新產品露營車 Evergreen 之發表會日期, 已決定於 9 月 22 日舉行。

　　除了將於電視與電臺的黃金時段播放全新廣告外, 並將在國內各大報上, 以全頁的廣告作宣傳。此外, 並已在史普蘭汀大飯店的別館預定了「彩虹廳」, 以舉行保證前所未有的驚奇產品發表會。

　　身為與本公司合作最久, 也最成功的經銷商之一, 為了向閣下對本公司榮景所作的貢獻致上無比之謝忱, 我們擬邀請您參與晚會最後的壓軸演出。

　　發表會的詳細內容, 本公司特別促銷部門的人員仍在策劃中, 但原則上, 我們計畫安排一臺 Evergreen, 由大廳的天花板緩緩降下, 從中出現預先乘坐在裏頭的幾位選美會中獲得優勝的美女, 再由美女向本公司最成功的三位經銷商獻花致敬。我們並安排了至少三家電視臺的攝影師實地錄影, 深信此發表會對本公司全體員工而言, 必將是個最具一流水準的廣告宣傳活動。

　　若您能出席此次新奇的產品發表會, 麻煩請與我們聯絡。

　　　　　　　　　　　　　　　　　　　　　　　　　　謹上

【語句注釋】◆ **launch**　「(新產品) 發表、發售」。此字當動詞時, 可用於火箭等的「發射」, 也可使用於新船的「下水典禮」, 即 a launching ceremony。新商品上市時, 也可以用 put something on the market 的說法。◆ **set for**　「決定 (時間、日期等)」。◆ **prime-time advertising slots**　「黃金時段播放的廣告」。slot 指節目播送的時段。advertising slot 指播放廣告的時段。◆ **a full-page spread**　「全頁的廣告」。◆ **for what promises to be**　「預計將～」。It promises to be a very interesting day.「預計將是個非常有趣的一天」。◆ **result in ～**　「導致～, 造成～的結果」。◆ **top-drawer publicity** 「一流水準的廣告宣傳活動」。

　　雖受到對方誠摯的邀請，卻覺得如自己一般的白髮老人，在如此盛大的發表會的最後壓軸節目出現，實有些唐突。詢問可否由該公司中較為年輕的適合人選代替，婉轉地謝絕出席發表會的一封信。

Dear Mr. Overton,

I'm honored that you should have invited me to take part in the product launch of your new trailer, but I'm afraid I'm getting a little too old for anything so, how shall I say—dramatic?

From your description, it certainly sounds as if it's going to be an exciting event. I feel reluctant to decline your kind invitation, but I do think that maybe someone a little younger would be more suitable.

Would it be possible for someone else to take my place? I can think of several young men in our Sales Department who would be far more photogenic than a gray-haired old man like myself.

Yours truly,

歐佛頓先生台鑒：

　　很榮幸能受邀出席貴公司新型露營車的發表會。然而本人深恐自己的年歲有些過大，是否不太適合參與如此…我該怎麼形容呢，…如此充滿戲劇性的新產品發表會？

　　由閣下邀請函中的描述，確實令人感受到此次發表會，必將是一令人興奮的活動。對閣下誠摯的邀請，實感萬難拒絕，不過，本人真的認為，或許由年紀較輕的人參加，會較為合適。

　　不知是否可由他人代替本人出席？本公司的業務部中，我認為有幾個年輕人，比起我這個白髮老人，還要來得上像得多。

　　　　　　　　　　　　　　　　　　　　　　　　　　　　　謹上

【語句注釋】◆ you should have invited 「受您的邀請」。雖也可只用 you have invited，但加入 should 後，有一種「確實決定邀請」的感覺。◆ it certainly sounds as if ～ 「確實令人覺得～」。◆ I feel reluctant to ～ 「苦於～，不願～」。◆ take my place 「代替我」。◆ photogenic 「上像的」。◆ a gray-haired old man 「白髮老人」。

【注意】回絕邀請之類信函的撰寫，要是沒有充分的理由將非常難以下筆。此信主要說明自己雖能接受對方的邀請，不過因自身年事已高，而希望辭退出席如此盛大的場面。也就是說，此決定乃基於個人多重的考量，故不但不失禮，還具有相當的說服力，應可獲得對方的諒解。

請求為開幕慶祝會剪綵的書信。

Madam:

The **grand opening ceremony** for our new Leamington superstore will take place at 10:00 am on Monday, March 21, and **we should be deeply honoured if Your Worship** could attend and perform the official opening.

The ceremony will begin with a short five-minute speech by Mr. Charles Baldwin, the President of Multisave U.K., and an **even shorter speech** by Mr. Fred Warrington, the manager of the new superstore. After these speeches there will be a **formal presentation** of bouquets, and we should like to ask you to say a few words before cutting the tape with a pair of **golden scissors**.

Very truly yours,

市長女士鈞鑒：

　　本公司雷明頓超市新分店的盛大開幕儀式，將在 3 月 21 日星期一上午 10 時舉行，若市長能撥空出席為小店主持正式的開幕儀式，本公司上下將深感無限光榮。

　　此開幕式將由英國毛堤塞伍公司總裁 —— 查爾斯‧鮑德溫先生約 5 分鐘的演說開始，接著再由新超市的經理 —— 佛瑞德‧渥林頓先生簡短地致詞。致詞之後，將有個正式的獻花儀式。我們希望市長女士能在持金剪刀剪綵之前，簡短地說幾句話。

　　　　　　　　　　　　　　　　　　　　　　　　　　　謹上

【語句注釋】◆ grand opening ceremony 「盛大的開幕典禮」。◆ we should be deeply honoured if ～ 「若～我們將深感光榮」。因採英式說法，故用 should 及 honoured；美式說法則普遍使用 we would be honored if ～。◆ Your Worship 「市長大人」。Worship 乃對市長等高位者的敬稱，Your Worship 在內容上與 you 相同。◆ even shorter speech 「更為簡短的致詞」。even 加強 shorter，表「更～」之意。still 的語義也大致相同。◆ formal presentation 「贈呈儀式」。formal 在此為「禮儀上的」之意。◆ golden scissors 「金剪刀」。scissors 通常加 -s 使用。例如：nippers, trousers。

剛到英國不久的商人，受邀出席其他公司的開幕慶祝會，詢問自己該穿什麼服裝以及該帶什麼禮物才好的信。

Dear Miss Roberts,

Many thanks for the invitation card I received for the gala opening of your company's new Birmingham showroom.

I shall be delighted to attend, and have already returned the acceptance postcard to your office.

To be honest, I have never attended such a gala opening, and am not sure about how to dress, or what to bring. Please let me know if there is anything that guests are expected to do on such occasions, or anything else you think I should be aware of.

I'm sorry to ask you such elementary questions, but I have been in the United Kingdom for only one month, and am still not familiar with the customs here.

Yours faithfully,

羅柏茲小姐台鑒:

　　衷心地感謝您寄來邀請參加貴公司位於伯明罕之新展示場的開幕慶祝會招待函。

　　我很樂意參加,並已寄出「出席」的明信片至您的辦公室。

　　不過老實說,我從來未曾參加過這類型的開幕慶祝會,不確定自己的服裝應如何穿著,或該帶什麼前往。在這樣子的場合,若有任何到場客人該做的、或者應該注意的地方,請您多多指教。

　　很抱歉寫信詢問如此基本的問題,實因本人方到英國 1 個月,尚未熟悉此地的習慣之故。

謹上

【語句注釋】◆ gala 「(公開)慶祝會」。gala opening 為「開幕慶祝會」之意。◆ shall be delighted to ～ 「很高興～」。delighted 和 glad 及 pleased 相比,雖較不為國人所熟悉,但卻是個令人感覺非常好的字彙。shall 在美國普遍用 will 代替。◆ acceptance postcard 「答應出席的明信片」。◆ be expected to ～ 「應做～,該注意～」。◆ on such occasions 「在如此的場合」。注意 occasion 前面的介系詞要用 on。◆ the United Kingdom 「英國」。正式名稱為 the United Kingdom of Great Britain and Northern Ireland,一般略作 UK。◆ still 「仍舊,依然」。◆ be familiar with ～ 「習慣於～,熟知～」。

此信答覆了關於開幕慶祝會的詢問（範例 2-4）。

Dear Mr. Anderson,

I was glad to hear that you will be coming to our gala opening, and I look forward to meeting you then.

Let me try and answer your questions one by one.

First, the reception following the official opening of the showroom will be a fairly informal affair. There will be lots of food and drink, and plenty of live music. Dress is completely optional, but I think you would probably feel a little out of place in a dark suit. Perhaps something a little more casual would fit the bill.

Second, I'm not sure what you mean about bringing things to the opening. We don't expect guests to bring anything. On the contrary, we hope they'll go home with many of the spot prizes we'll be offering during the party.

As for what you should do during the party, the simple answer is, "Enjoy yourself!" Guests will be moving around a lot, eating, drinking, and meeting one another.

I hope this puts your mind at rest. If you have any other questions, why don't you call me directly? You can reach me during office hours by dialing 0171-543-0392 and asking for Extension 450.

Yours faithfully,

安德森先生台鑒：

　　很高興獲悉閣下將出席本公司之開幕慶祝會，期待在會場上與您見面。

　　讓我試著在此逐一回答閣下的問題。

　　首先，緊接著展示場開幕儀式之後，是一個相當簡單、非正式的餐會。有許多食物、飲料、以及現場演奏的音樂。服裝上完全自由，不過深色系的西裝，也許會有些格格不入。或許「較輕便」的服飾，將會比較適合。

　　第二，我不太確定您信中提及的帶東西到會場一事，是什麼意思。我們並不期待客人帶來任何東西。相反的，我們希望每個客人回家時，能帶回許多我們在慶祝會中所提供的獎品。

　　至於閣下在晚會中該做什麼？最簡單的回答是「盡興」。所有的客人將四處走動，吃吃喝喝及交談。

　　希望以上的回覆能使閣下放鬆心情。若您還有任何其他問題，何不直接撥電話給我？您可於辦公時間撥 0171–543–0392 轉分機 450 就能找到我。

　　　　　　　　　　　　　　　　　　　　　　　　　　　　謹上

【語句注釋】◆ gala　參照範例 2–4。◆ feel out of place　「無法融入情境中」。◆ something a little more casual　「較輕便的～」。指 something that is a little more casual。◆ fit the bill　「合乎標準」。也可使用 fill the bill。◆ put your mind at rest「使閣下放鬆心情」。也可說成 set your heart at ease。

2-6 參觀全面更新設備的工廠的通知

　　全面更新設備的工廠將為代理商安排一次新設備的參觀行程。因須事前準備且有人數上的限制，希望有意參觀者能在截止日期前與其聯絡的一封信。

Dear Mr. Coniston,

I am pleased to inform you that **the re-tooling of our** Tainan **Plant** is now complete, and the plant should **go into full operation** on Monday, February 5.

A number of our **distributors** have **expressed interest in** the new facility, and we **have decided to** arrange **a plant tour** for approximately 15–20 participants.

If you would like to **take part in** this tour, and see **for yourself** the new equipment we have installed, could you please let me know by January 25 at the latest.

Yours sincerely,

柯尼斯頓先生台鑒：

　　很榮幸地在此向您報告，臺南工廠全面更新設備的作業已經完成，而且本工廠將於 2 月 5 日星期一全面開工。

　　因多家代理商表示有興趣參觀新設備，本公司已決定安排一次大約十五至二十人參加的參觀行程。

　　若您希望參加此次參觀行程，親眼目睹我們新引進的全新設備，請最遲於 1 月 25 日之前與我聯絡。

　　　　　　　　　　　　　　　　　　　　　　　　謹上

【語句注釋】◆ the re-tooling of our plant 「本公司工廠的全面更新設備」。◆ go into full operation 「全面動工」。◆ a number of distributors 「許多的代理商」。但是，a number of 有「許多」以及「若干」兩種意思，必須從前後文來判斷。(a number of) +（複數名詞）為主詞時，以複數動詞相對應。◆ express interest in ～ 「對～表示興趣」。express 為較文言的表現，show interest in 則較為口語化。◆ have decided to ～ 「決定～」。◆ a plant tour 「參觀工廠的行程」。也稱 a factory tour。tour 指「巡迴，視察」，故有「參觀實習」之意。◆ take part in ～ 「參加～」。◆ for yourself 「親自地」。for oneself「自己為了自己，獨力地」之意。相對地，by oneself 則有「只有自己，全靠自己一人」的意思。

3

介紹信函

3–1　介紹信（拜託機場接機）

　　同事初次到日本，萬事皆備，獨對如何由機場到東京市區下榻飯店一事，仍有些許不安。自己上回赴日，對方公司派人到機場接機令其印象深刻，故委託對方為其同事做相同的安排。

Dear Mr. Carter,

My colleague Bernard Ripley will be traveling to Japan next month, and hopes to visit your office within a few days of his arrival. He will, of course, contact you beforehand and arrange a mutually convenient time.

This is his first visit to Japan. Although his secretary has taken care of all transport and accommodation details, he still feels a little uneasy about getting to his hotel in Tokyo from the airport.

You may remember that the last time I myself visited Japan, you kindly arranged for someone from your office to meet me at Narita Airport and accompany me into town. I wonder if you could possibly extend the same courtesy to Bernard. I know he would appreciate it very much.

Please do not hesitate to tell me if this causes you any inconvenience. I know how busy your office always is, and I am fully aware how difficult it is to spare someone for most of one day.

Yours sincerely,

卡特先生台鑒：

　　我的同事柏納‧雷普利將於下個月到日本，並希望在他抵達後的數天內，到貴公司拜訪。當然，他會事先與您聯繫，安排一個雙方都合適的時間。

　　這是他初次造訪日本，雖然祕書已辦妥了各項交通、住宿等細節，但他本人仍有些擔心，不知如何由機場到東京市區下榻的飯店。

　　或許您還記得，上回我到日本拜訪時，承蒙您熱心的安排，派了公司的人到成田機場接機，並一路伴隨著我到市區。不知此回是否也能為柏納作相同的安排？相信他將十分感激。

　　若此要求造成您有所不便，請不要猶豫，千萬要告訴我。我很了解貴公司業務繁忙，也完全明白要安排某人騰出將近一整天的時間接機並伴隨回市區是很困難的事情。

謹上

【語句注釋】◆ colleague 「同事」。◆ contact you beforehand 「事先與您聯絡」。◆ all transport and accommodation details 「所有交通及住宿的相關細節」。◆ you kindly arranged for someone to meet me 「承蒙您好意地安排人來接我」。◆ extend the same courtesy to ～ 「給予～同樣的善意」。courtesy「優厚的對待，好意，特別的照顧」。◆ Please do not hesitate to ～ 「請別猶豫～」。同樣的意思，也可用 Please feel free to ～來表示。◆ spare someone 「騰出、撥出某人（的時間）」。We can spare him for tomorrow.「他明天不在也沒有關係」。spare 通常指「撥出金錢、時間」的情況較多。Can you spare me a few minutes?「可否佔用您幾分鐘的時間?」

應範例 3-1 的請託，允諾一定派人接機，故希望對方告知班機號碼以及抵達時間。若能告知飯店名稱，將可代為查詢是否有無機場到飯店的巴士接送服務等內容的回函。

Dear Mr. Watson,

I shall of course be delighted to arrange for someone to meet your colleague Mr. Bernard Ripley at Narita Airport.

If you could ask his secretary to fax us his flight number and arrival time, I will **make sure that** someone is there to meet him when he **clears customs**.

It would also help if you could let us know at which hotel he will be staying. **There may be a** direct limousine **bus service available**, and that would probably be the most comfortable, **if not necessarily** the quickest, route into town.

Please let us know **if there is any other way we can be of help to you** or Mr. Ripley.

Yours sincerely,

華特森先生台鑒：

　　當然我很樂意安排專人到成田機場迎接您的同事柏納‧雷普利先生。您若能請他的祕書以傳真通知我們他的班機號碼以及抵達時間，我保證將派人在機場出關的地方迎接他。

　　此外，您若能告訴我們他預定住宿的飯店名稱，將有助於我們詢問是否有直接從機場到飯店的巴士接送服務。此法雖不一定是最快速進入市區的方式，不過卻是最舒適的。

　　若有任何我們可以協助您或雷普利先生的地方，請不吝告知。

謹上

【語句注釋】◆ make sure that ～　「一定～，保證～」。◆ clear customs　「出海關」。◆ it would help if you could ～　「若能～將大有助益」。◆ There is a bus service available　「有巴士接送服務」。available「能利用，能取得」。◆ if not necessarily ～　「雖不一定～，即使不～也」。◆ if there is any other way we can be of help to you　「若有其他可協助的地方」。

因應營業人員的調職而介紹繼任者的一封信。

Dear Mr. Smith:

This letter is to introduce Ms. Erika Ando of our Setagaya Sales Office.

Ms. Ando has taken over the position of sales consultant for the Komazawa Park area from Ms. Yukiko Watanabe who, as you may know, transferred to our Hachioji Customer Support Office in March.

Ms. Ando has been with All-Fresh for over five years, and is one of our most experienced sales consultants. She will be only too pleased to assist you in any way possible, and will call on you in person in the very near future.

She will bring with her a special preview catalog of the exciting new line of electronic air purifiers we shall be launching this summer.

Sincerely yours,

史密斯先生台鑒：

　　茲以此信向您介紹本公司世田谷營業處的安藤繪里香小姐。

　　如閣下所知悉，因渡邊悠紀子小姐已於 3 月調職至八王子的顧客服務中心，故由安藤小姐繼任負責駒澤公園地區之營業顧問的職務。

　　安藤小姐服務於全鮮公司已超過 5 年，並為本公司最資深的營業顧問之一。她將很樂意盡她所能在各方面協助您，並於近期內親自登門造訪。

　　屆時她將帶給您本公司今年夏天即將問世的新型電子空氣清淨機的特別預告目錄。

謹上

【語句注譯】 ◆ **This letter is to introduce** ～　「茲以此信（向您）介紹～」。此乃用於介紹信時的固定句型。◆ **take over**　「繼任」。◆ **transfer**　「轉任，調職」。在此乃表示「移動」的不及物動詞，transfer 也可使用為「使調職」的及物動詞。用作及物動詞時，需以 who was transferred 之被動語態表示。◆ **Ms. Ando has been with All-Fresh**　「安藤小姐服務於全鮮已～」。此時，with 所連用的名詞表示所服務的公司。◆ **in any way possible**　「儘可能地，以任何方式～」。即「竭盡全力地～」之意。◆ **in person**　「本人，直接」。不透過電話或代理人，而由本人親自接洽。◆ **preview**　「預告，預覽」。

因自己的公司沒有顧客所查詢的商品而推薦其他公司的一封信。

Dear Mr. Smith,

Many thanks for your **enquiry** about the **installation** of an electronic **anti-theft** system in your new car.

We do not **carry** this particular line of automobile **equipment**, but will be happy to introduce a **reputable** dealer in your area.

Shin-Shin Motors of 51, Lane 272, Fushing North Road specialize in the kind of item you are looking for, and we are sure they will be able to **satisfy your requirements**.

They can be **reached** at 2789–3110, and their fax number is 2789–3119.

Yours sincerely,

史密斯先生台鑒：

　　很感謝閣下對新車裝設電子防盜系統的查詢。

　　很遺憾的，本公司並沒有銷售此項特別的汽車配備，不過我們將很樂於向您介紹您住處附近的一家深受好評的經銷商。

　　位於復興北路 272 巷 51 號的欣欣汽車正是您所查詢之配備的專門店，我們確定他們必定能滿足您的需求。

　　您可以電話 2789–3110 或傳真 2789–3119 與該公司聯絡。

謹上

【語句注釋】◆ enquiry 「查詢，詢問」。原本 enquiry（查詢，詢問）與 inquiry（調查，研究）二個動詞分別表達不同的意思，不過在美國，上述二者皆以 inquiry 表示。最近在英國的商業界亦愈來愈趨向此用法。◆ installation 「設置，裝設」。◆ anti-theft 「防（止竊）盜」。◆ carry 「（商家）為了銷售而持有」。◆ equipment 「配備，工具」。注意 equipment 通常為不可數名詞。◆ reputable 「深受好評的，名聲好的」。◆ satisfy your requirements 「滿足閣下的需求」。也可說成 meet your requirements。◆ reach 「（以電話等）聯絡」。

3-5 介紹信（介紹同事）

因臨時有事無法會見原本約定商談投資事宜的顧客，向顧客說明請同事代為洽談的一封信。

Dear Mr. Dawson,

I am sorry to say that I shall be out of town on Tuesday, June 21, and will therefore be unable to meet you on that day.

I have arranged for my colleague John Hampton to go in my place, and have briefed him thoroughly on your investment portfolio.

John has been with M. W. Finance for more than five years, and is one of our most experienced consultants. You can discuss your investment plans with him in full confidence, and he will report back to me when I return to Aston next week.

Apologies for any inconvenience this sudden change may cause you.

Yours faithfully,

道森先生台鑒：

　　因 6 月 21 日星期二有事必須到外地去，故是日無法與您會面，對此我深感抱歉。

　　我已安排由同事約翰‧漢普頓暫代我的職務，並已詳細地向他介紹您的投資明細。

　　約翰服務於 M. W. 財經已超過 5 年，為本公司最資深的顧問之一。您儘可放心地與他討論您的投資計畫，當我下個禮拜返回艾斯頓時，他將向我報告與您討論的經過。

　　謹在此為此突發的變更所帶來的不便之處向您致歉。

　　　　　　　　　　　　　　　　　　　　　　　　　　　謹上

【語句注釋】◆ colleague 「同事」。◆ in ～'s place 「替代某人」。◆ brief 「詳細說明」。在此為動詞。◆ portfolio 在此指特定的個人、機關團體所持有的各種有價證券的明細一覽表。◆ John has been with M.W. Finance ～ 「約翰已服務於 M.W. 財經（顧問公司）～」。在此 with 指「服務於～」。（請參照範例 3-3 的【語句注釋】）◆ discuss your investment plans 「討論您的投資計畫」。discuss 因為及物動詞，故為 discuss ～，而不是 discuss about ～。例如：He discussed his investment plans with Mr. Hampton. ◆ cause inconvenience 「造成不便之處」。與 give trouble 相較，cause inconvenience 感覺語氣較和緩。

4

感謝函

　　告知自己平安返國，感謝停留期間受到多方照顧的致謝函。（參見範例 5–1～5–5）

Dear Mr. Jenkins,

I returned to Taipei on Friday evening, and **was back at work** this morning.

I want to thank you for the warm hospitality you extended to me during my visit to England. I thoroughly enjoyed our game of golf, and your wife's cooking was, as usual, simply marvellous. I also enjoyed meeting your neighbours, Mr. and Mrs. Banerjee. They are such a delightful couple, and I think you are very fortunate to have such wonderful people living next door to you.

I am not sure how I can possibly **repay** you for your kindness. Please remember that, **should you ever come to Taiwan**, my home is your home. Linda and I would welcome the opportunity to show you around Taipei, or any other places you'd like to visit.

Please give my best regards to Mrs. Jenkins. I am enclosing copies of some photos I took at your house. I'm afraid they are not very good (I have never **been handy with** a camera), but I hope they serve as a small **reminder** of the enjoyable time we spent together.

Yours sincerely,

詹金斯先生台鑒：

　　我已於星期五晚間返抵臺北，並於今晨返回工作崗位。

　　非常感謝此次在英國的訪問期間，受到您熱誠地款待。與閣下的高爾夫球賽，可說極為盡興。此外，尊夫人的手藝，一如往常，好得沒話說。也很榮幸地，能與您的鄰居柏納紀先生夫人見面。他們是一對如此開朗的夫婦，您實在很幸運能與這麼好的人為鄰。

　　真不知如何才能回報您的熱情款待。請千萬記得，若您有機會來到臺灣，請把我家當作您自己的家。琳達和我將很高興能有機會帶您參觀臺北，或其他您想去的地方。

　　請代我向尊夫人致上最真誠的問候。信內附上幾張我在您的住處拍攝的照片。很遺憾拍得並不十分完美（我一向對相機外行），不過希望它們能為我們所共度的快樂時光留下紀念。

　　　　　　　　　　　　　　　　　　　　　　　　　　　　謹上

【語句注釋】◆ **be back at work** 「回到工作崗位」。back 為返回（原來的場所、狀態）之意的副詞。be at work 指在職務工作，與 back 合用，變成「出差回來，開始工作」。◆ **repay** 「回禮，回報，報恩」。也經常使用 reciprocate 來表達同樣的意思。◆ **should you ever come to Taiwan** 「若您有機會來訪臺灣時」。◆ **be handy with ～** 「內行～，擅於～」。a handy person「手巧的人」。◆ **reminder** 「紀念之物，喚起回憶的東西」。

4-1 對受訪者熱情款待的感謝函　65

對範例 4-1 的回函。單就對方能到自己家來，全家已感到非常高興，告訴對方不要掛念在心上的一封溫暖貼心的信。

Dear Mr. Liu,

I can imagine how busy you must be after your return from your business trip to England, and I appreciate your taking the time to write to me on your first day back at work.

The photographs were a pleasant surprise. How did you manage to get them developed so quickly? You say that you're not very handy with a camera, but the photos are excellent. Deborah was so pleased with the three photos that you took in our garden that she plans to frame them and hang them in our living room.

Please understand that it was our pleasure to have you visit us here in Wormsley, and I would hate to think that you now feel yourself under some kind of obligation to us.

Deborah and I truly appreciate your offer to show us around Taipei, but somehow I feel that our dream of visiting Taiwan is slipping further and further away. We're not getting any younger, and it's getting more difficult to get out and about.

Please give our fondest regards to your wife Linda, and our congratulations to your daughter on the birth of her first baby.

Yours sincerely,

劉先生台鑒：

　　我可以想像，您自英國洽公之行回到工作崗位之後該有多麼忙碌，並謝謝您在回到工作後的第一天即撥空寫信給我。

　　您寄來的照片真是個意外的驚喜。您怎麼這麼快就沖洗出照片？您說您對相機外行，在我看來這些照片都棒極了。黛博拉好喜歡您在我們家花園中拍攝的三張照片，並打算裱框掛在家中的客廳。

　　希望您了解到，能有您到訪我們溫斯利的家中，是我們的榮幸，千萬不要有任何虧欠我們人情的感覺。

　　黛博拉和我很感謝您提及要帶我們參觀臺北一事，只不過我感覺此拜訪臺灣的夢想是離我們愈來愈遠了。我們已不復年輕，出門遠行也愈來愈困難。

　　請代我們向夫人琳達獻上最衷心的問候，並恭賀令嬡初獲麟兒。

謹上

【語句注釋】◆ a pleasant surprise 　「意外的驚喜」。◆ frame 　「裝入相框」。◆ have you visit us 　「您的大駕光臨」。用 have + 受格 + 不定詞原形的方式表示（人）受到（受格的人）來訪。例如：We had many guests visit us.（我們有許多客人來訪。）◆ you feel under obligation to us 　「您覺得虧欠我們人情」。◆ slip away 　「在不知不覺中消失，不知何時消逝無蹤」。

致上訪美時受招待的感謝函的同時，附上謝禮招福貓一座為主旨的信。

Dear Ms. Mortimer,

I returned to Tokyo on March 18, after a long but **uneventful** flight from Seattle.

I consider myself extremely fortunate to have **made your acquaintance** during my brief stay in Denver. I truly appreciate the time and effort you took to show me around the town, and the wonderful dinner to which you invited me afterwards.

As a very small token of my appreciation, I am sending you a Japanese "maneki-neko" doll. It represents a cat inviting **good fortune** to come and visit the home, office, or shop in which it is placed. I do hope that you like the doll, and that it will bring you good luck in the future.

Although I did not meet your family, I feel as if I know them very well, thanks to the many photographs you showed me. Please give them my best regards, and please let me know if there is anyway that I might possibly **be of service to** you.

Yours sincerely,

摩提米爾小姐惠鑒：

　　從西雅圖一路平安的長途飛行之後，我已於 3 月 18 日返抵東京。
　　在丹佛的短期停留中，深感十分的幸運，能與您相識。同時也感
激您花了這麼多寶貴的時間和精神，帶領我參觀市區，又在當晚招待
我如此豐盛的晚餐。
　　為表示我的感謝，隨函附上一座日本的「招福貓」以為紀念。它
是一種能招引好運到家庭、辦公室或商店的幸運物。希望您喜歡並帶
給您好運。
　　此行雖然沒能會見您的家人，不過從您讓我看的照片，就能感覺
自己與他們有如舊識一般。請代我向家人獻上最誠摯的祝福，若有任
何我能為您效勞之處，亦請不吝告知。

　　　　　　　　　　　　　　　　　　　　　　　　　　謹上

【語句注釋】 ◆ **uneventful** 「沒有變化；沒什麼特別的事」。在此指「一路平安無
事」。 ◆ **make ～'s acquaintance** 「認識～」。也可用 make acquaintance of ～。 ◆ **as a
very small token of my appreciation** 「作為小小的感謝之紀念」。英語中也有如此的謙
虛表現。 ◆ **good fortune** 「幸運」。和後來出現的 good luck 同義。 ◆ **be of service to
～** 「有益於～」。用於自己有助益於對方的場合。因此，若向對方說 Please be of service
to us. 則非常失禮。

在國外遺失貴重的東西，因已沒有希望能找回，心情幾乎跌入絕望的谷底。然而，當失物出乎意料地失而復得時，正因為早已不抱任何希望了，那份喜悅更是非同小可。此封信是為了向拾獲失物的人表達難以言喻的感激之情而寫的感謝函。

Dear Ms. suzuki,

I returned home this evening to find your parcel waiting for me in the hall.

Imagine my surprise and delight to find that it contained the Filofax I **mislaid in Tokyo**. I had been **racking my brains trying to remember** where I last used it, and where I might possibly have lost it.

You say that one of your receptionists found it behind one of the armchairs in the lobby of your building. I **am** greatly **indebted to** her for finding it, and would like to send her **a small token of my gratitude**. Could you let me have her **full name** and, if possible, her home address?

Thank you once again for sending the Filofax back to me. I **was** truly **lost without** it.

Sincerely yours,

鈴木小姐惠鑒：

　　今晚回到家中時，赫然在玄關發現您寄來的包裹。

　　您可想像，當我發現包裹中有我在東京遺失的活頁記事本時是多麼地吃驚與欣喜。發現它不見之後，我絞盡腦汁，試著回憶我最後使用的地點，以及最可能遺落的地方。

　　您提及貴公司的接待員，在大廳的一座椅後面發現我的活頁記事本。我極為感激她的這份恩情，並希望寄給她本人一份小禮以表示我的感激。不知可否告訴我她的全名，如果可能的話，可否連同她家裡的住址一併告訴我。

　　再次感謝您寄回我的活頁記事本。沒有它，我實在不知如何是好。

　　　　　　　　　　　　　　　　　　　　　　　　謹上

【語句注釋】◆ **mislaid in Tokyo** 「在東京遺失」。mislay 為「丟失 (lose)」的婉轉表達用法。◆ **rack my brains** 「拼命地想，絞盡腦汁」。◆ **try to remember** 「努力使自己想起」不可說成 try remembering。通常 try 之後接不定詞或動名詞時，語義不同。例如：try to eat onion（努力地使自己敢吃洋蔥）、try eating onion（試吃洋蔥），須分辨清楚。◆ **be indebted to～** 「受到～之恩、欠～恩情」。◆ **a small token of my gratitude** 「小小的謝禮」。token 有「紀念品、土產」和「象徵、紀念」的二種意義。在此含有雙重意義。此外，也有 by the same token（此外；因而聯想起；基於此證據）的片語。◆ **full name** 「全名」。在西方，first, middle, last name 總稱為 full name。即「姓名」。◆ **be lost without～** 「沒有了～不知如何是好」。

在契約期限之前提前離職，通常都相當地困難。不過，有幸能遇到好的上司，得以圓滿地退職，對此恭敬地表示謝意的致謝函。

Dear Mr. Mori:

Earlier today I received a telephone call from Mr. Frampton of **Allied Investments**, informing me that he had spoken to you **in person**, and that you **had no objections to** my leaving **Kitamura Finance** and moving to Allied Investments.

I wanted to write and thank you for your **magnanimity** in allowing me to leave before the expiration of my contract.

I have **enjoyed working** at Kitamura, and will always remember my friends and colleagues with much pleasure and affection.

Yours faithfully,

摩利先生賜鑒：

　　今天稍早我接到聯盟投資的佛蘭普頓先生的來電，他告訴我他本人已親自和您談過，並提及您對我離開北村金融轉往聯盟投資一事，沒有任何異議。

　　在此謹以書面向您感謝您的寬大，允許我在契約期限未滿前離開。

　　很高興能在北村金融工作，也將時時懷念在此的所有朋友與同事。

謹上

【語句注釋】◆ **Allied Investment** 「聯盟投資」。「投資公司」是以投資為目的，持有其他公司股票的公司。與此相關的「控股公司」則指非以投資為目的，為了控制他公司之企業活動，而持有他公司股份的公司。◆ **in person** 「親自地，本人直接」。◆ **have no objections to ～** 「對～毫無異議」。◆ **Kitamura Finance** 「北村金融」。金融公司名。◆ **magnanimity** 「寬大，雅量」。magnanimities 指寬容的行為。◆ **enjoy working** 「愉快地工作」。enjoy 後接動名詞為受詞，不接不定詞。此類動詞有很多，以基本的動詞為例，如 mind, escape, give up, avoid, finish, enjoy, put off, stop, 可用各片語的字頭字母，記憶為 MEGAFEPS。

5

訪　問

告知對方目前祕書正在排定行程，預計此次將會前去倫敦出差，期待屆時能再相聚的短信。

Dear Mr. Jenkins,

I shall be in England **on business** next month, and would **welcome** an opportunity to meet with you again.

My secretary should finalize my itinerary within the next few days, and I will let you know **my dates in London** as soon as I have them.

I hope **all is well** with you and your family. Please give my best regards to **your good wife**.

Yours sincerely,

詹金斯先生台鑒：

　　我將於下個月到英國出差，並希望能有機會再次與您會面。
　　我的祕書將在數日內最後確定行程。屆時，我會立即通知您，我在倫敦停留的日期。
　　希望您和家人一切如意。並請代我向您的賢內助問候。

　　　　　　　　　　　　　　　　　　　　　　　　　　　　　謹上

【語句注釋】◆ on business 「因公出差」。go abroad on business（海外出差）。此外，
注意人也經常使用 be on loan to ～（到～出差）。例如，He is on loan to their subsidiary in
Hong Kong.（他出差到香港的分公司）。通常為銀行用語。◆ welcome 「樂於接受」。
◆ my dates in London 「我在倫敦停留的日期」。◆ all is well 「萬事順利」。All's
Well that Ends Well.（事事圓滿）（莎士比亞的劇作）。◆ your good wife 「賢內助」。
good「品德良好的」。

5-1　預定到訪的通知　77

內容包括非常高興對方下個月的來訪，告知自己除了第一個禮拜不在之外，之後的行程皆可彈性調整。自己的妻子也很期待對方的來訪，並報告近況。

Dear Mr. Liu,

I was delighted to hear that you'll be coming to London next month. I shall be **out of town** during the first week of the month, but **apart from** that my schedule is fairly flexible.

I know you're a very busy man, but I hope that this time you'll be able to **take** at least **one** whole **day off work**, and that we'll be able to enjoy a round of golf together.

Deborah has now recovered almost completely from a fall she had when she was **redecorating** the children's bedroom. The **stepladder** she was standing on slipped, and she took a rather bad **tumble**. The doctors removed the **plaster cast** ten days ago, and the **cut** she **sustained** on her arm has healed completely. She insists that you come over for dinner, and asks if you have any special requests.

Please let me know your dates in London as soon as you have them.

Yours sincerely,

劉先生台鑒:

　　非常高興您將於下個月來到倫敦。我除了第一個禮拜因事需離開倫敦外，大致的行程都可彈性調整。

　　我知道您相當忙碌，不過我希望此行您能休個一整天的假，屆時我們可以一起愉快地打一場高爾夫球。

　　黛博拉前陣子在重新裝修小孩的房間時，不小心跌倒，不過現已大致復原。她從梯子上滑了一跤，整個身子重重地摔了下來。醫生已於 10 天前拆掉了石膏，手臂上的割傷也已完全痊癒。她堅持要您來家中共進晚餐，並詢問您是否有任何特別的要求。

　　日期決定後，請馬上和我們聯絡。

　　　　　　　　　　　　　　　　　　　　　　　　　　　　　謹上

【語句注釋】◆ out of town 「離開城市」。◆ apart from ～ 「除～之外」。◆ take one day off work 「休一天的假」。◆ redecorate 「重新裝潢」。◆ stepladder 「四腳梯，梯凳」。◆ tumble 「跌倒，摔倒」。◆ plaster cast 「用以固定的石膏」。◆ cut 「傷口，切傷」。◆ sustain 「損傷，受傷」。通常用作「支持，維持」之意較多，在此指「受傷」，須注意。

　　行程已底定。抵英之後的第一個禮拜，自己也將忙於工作，之後的週末應可一起揮桿打高爾夫球。得知夫人意外受傷，除深表遺憾外，也為其復原感到高興。針對範例 5-2 傳達上述內容之回信。

Dear Mr. Jenkins,

Many thanks for your letter of September 10.

My secretary tells me that she has now made all the necessary reservations for my trip to England. I shall be arriving in London on October 3, and staying for two weeks.

In addition to several appointments I have with clients and business partners in London, I have to make two short trips to Manchester and Carlisle. I shall try to fit these trips into the first week of my stay, and at the moment it looks as if I should be free on the weekend of October 12–13.

I was sorry to hear about your wife's accident. I told my wife, Linda, about it, and she was most upset. We're happy to hear, however, that she's recovering well.

I'd love to come and have dinner with you, but are you sure that it won't be too much trouble for your wife?

Yours sincerely,

詹金斯先生台鑒：

　　謝謝您於 9 月 10 日寄來的信。

　　我的祕書告訴我，她現已完全為我安排好此趟英國之行的所有預約工作。我將於 10 月 3 日抵達倫敦，停留 2 個禮拜。

　　除了在倫敦，將有幾個與客戶和生意上的夥伴的會談外，我還必須到曼徹斯特和卡來爾二地。我將盡可能將這些旅行安排在停留期間的第一個禮拜。照目前的行程看來，10 月 12–13 日的週末，我應該有空。

　　很遺憾聽到夫人意外受傷。當我告訴我太太琳達時，她更是難過。不過，我們也很高興得知，她復原得很好。

　　我將很高興能與您共進晚餐，但真的不會帶給夫人太多麻煩嗎？

　　　　　　　　　　　　　　　　　　　　　　　　　　　　　謹上

【語句注釋】◆ fit … into ～　「使配合；將…安置於～」。◆ at the moment　「目前」。此片語用於現在式時，指「現在、目前」，用於過去式時，則成為「當時」的意思。I arrived at the moment he was leaving.（當他正要離開時，我剛好抵達）。◆ upset　「心煩意亂的，不安的」。◆ I'd love to ～　「願意～，樂於～」。"Will you join us?" "I'd love to."（「你要不要加入我們？」「當然（很樂意）」）。

很高興此次到家裡的來訪，能有相當充裕的時間，並告知 10 月 12 日或 13 日都可以，並建議暫定以 13 日來訪的回函。

Dear Mr. Liu,

Thank you for your letter of September 15.

I was happy to hear that the schedule of your upcoming visit to England will **allow you enough time** to come and visit us here in Wormsley. I've checked with Deborah, and either October 12 or 13 is fine with us.

Might I suggest that we make it October 13? If you could come over around noon, we could have a light lunch and then drive over to the golf course and **fit in a leisurely round before tea**.

You didn't say whether you had any special requests for dinner. Deborah remembers how much you enjoyed her lamb cutlets the last time you visited us, and wonders if you'd like the same again.

Will you be staying at your usual hotel in London? If so, I'll give you a call as soon as I get back to London from my trip to Brussels.

I'm looking forward to seeing you again very soon.

Yours sincerely,

劉先生台鑒：

　　已收到您 9 月 15 日的來信。

　　很高興得知您此回的英國之行，能有充裕的時間，來到位在溫斯利的家中。我已知會黛博拉，原則上 10 月 12 日或 13 日，我們都有空。

　　我可否建議暫定為 10 月 13 日呢？若您能在正午左右到達，我們可有個簡單的午餐，然後驅車前往高爾夫球場，在下午茶之前輕鬆地打一場球。

　　您並未在信中提及晚餐有任何特別想吃的菜。黛博拉記得上次您很喜歡她準備的小羊排，不知您是否希望再嚐一次。

　　您將在倫敦投宿於同樣的飯店嗎？若是如此，在我由布魯塞爾回到倫敦後，將馬上打電話給您。

　　期待很快能與您見面。

　　　　　　　　　　　　　　　　　　　　　　　　　　　　謹上

【語句注釋】◆ **allow you enough time** 「（預定中）有充裕的時間」。allow ＋ 人 ＋ 名詞時，allow 與 give 皆具「給與」之意。allow ＋（人）＋ to do 時，則為「允許」之意。Allow me to introduce my friend Mr. White to you.（容我介紹我的朋友懷特先生。）
◆ **fit in** 「將～安置、調整入（預定計劃）」。◆ **a leisurely round** 「輕鬆地打一場球」。◆ **before tea** 「在下午茶時間前」。在英國下午 5 點鐘左右，有一邊吃茶點，一邊喝紅茶的習慣稱作 afternoon tea，也稱為 five-o'clock tea。

對方詢問可否將招待日期定於 10 月 13 日時，無論自己再如何忙碌，即便是簡短的幾句話，也務必要回覆。暫且按捺住雀躍的心情容見面再敘，首先必須告知所建議日期的可否。

Dear Mr. Jenkins,

Just a brief note to thank you for your letter of September 21, and to let you know that I'll be delighted to come and visit you on October 13.

I'm looking forward to playing golf with you at the beautiful Wormsley Golf Course, and I'm also looking forward to enjoying your wife's wonderful cooking again. Lamb cutlets would be most acceptable!

Yours sincerely,

詹金斯先生台鑒：

　　以簡單的幾句話，感謝您於 9 月 21 日寄來的信。並在此告知我將很榮幸地於 10 月 13 日登門造訪。

　　我非常期待和您在美麗的溫斯利高爾夫球場上打一場球，以及再次享用夫人的美味佳餚。小羊排，再好不過！

謹上

【語句注釋】◆ a brief note to ～　「（為了表示謝意時）簡短的幾句話～」。to thank you 及 to let you know 這二個不定詞片語，用來修飾 a brief note。

【注意】大家都知道凡事「稍加確認」是很重要的事，然而在忙碌時，這看似「丁點兒的」小事，卻常顯得相當困難。特別是商務上，有時一時的疏忽忘了「稍加確認」，事後往往演變成不可收拾的局面。因此，盡可能地使自己習慣於書寫此類的 a brief note。

5-5　對建議日期的回信　85

5-6　女兒前往拜訪的通知

6月即將從大學畢業的女兒，計畫和友人到歐洲畢業旅行。希望女兒若到對方住所附近的話，能前往拜訪一事，徵詢對方是否方便的信件。

Dear Mr. Campbell:

My daughter Lily will be graduating from National Taiwan University in June, and will take up a position with ABC Incorporated here in Taiwan from July 1st.

She has a few weeks to spare between the end of her final exams in May and the graduation ceremony in June, and she plans on taking a short trip to Europe with her best friend Joan.

Although their itinerary is still a little vague, the two girls should be in England at the beginning of June, and they want to see as much of the country as possible in the short time they have available. I told them that if they were going to travel to the Lake District, they should stop off in Derby and say hello to you and your wife. Do you think this would be possible?

Do you remember Mrs. Laing of the R&D Department? When I mentioned to her that I was going to write to you, she asked me to pass on her very best regards. She said she still uses the brass paperweight you gave her as a souvenir.

Yours sincerely,

坎貝爾先生大鑒：

　　我女兒莉莉將在6月份自國立臺灣大學畢業，並將自7月1日起任
職於臺北的ABC公司。

　　她自5月畢業考試結束到6月的畢業典禮之間，有2、3個禮拜的
空閒時間，故與好友瓊安計畫到歐洲作一趟簡短的旅行。

　　行程目前雖然還未完全確定，不過她們兩個女孩，應會在6月初
時停留在英國，並希望能在允許的短時間內，盡可能地遍遊全英國。
我告訴她們，若經過大湖區時，應到德貝向您和夫人問好。不知您覺
得是否可行？

　　您還記得研發部門的梁女士嗎？當我向她提及我將寫信給您時，
她希望我代為向您問好。她說她一直使用著您送給她的銅製文鎮紀念
品。

謹上

【語句注釋】◆ available 「可利用的，可使用的」。◆ the Lake District 「大湖
區」。位於英格蘭西北部，多湖水的山岳地帶。◆ stop off 「順道拜訪」。drop 也可表示
相同的意思。例如：drop in at Jimmy's（順道到吉米家拜訪）、drop by one's office（順便
拜訪某人的辦公室）。I just dropped by to say hello.（我只是進來打聲招呼）。◆ say hello
「打招呼，問好」。Please say hello to your wife.「請向夫人問好」。◆ R&D Department
「研究開發 (= Research and Development) 部門」。◆ pass on 「傳達」。Please pass on my
best regards.（請代我轉達問候之意）。

5-6 女兒前往拜訪的通知 87

非常歡迎令嬡及其好友的來訪。因須稍作準備，請在事前一個禮拜再行聯絡等相關內容的回信。

Dear Eric:

Your letter was such a nice surprise.

Just the other day I was saying to Ethel that we should write to you soon, and congratulate you on the promotion you mentioned in your Christmas card.

So your daughter is coming to England, is she? Ethel and I would **be thrilled** to **have her** and her friend **come and stay** with us for a day or two. If the girls don't mind **sharing**, they could have use of Tom's room on the first floor. Or if they prefer separate rooms, we could move a **camp bed** into **the spare room** on the second.

Do I remember Mrs. Laing? Of course I do! She is such a warm and friendly person, and she looked after me so well during my visit to your plant. Please give her my fondest regards, and please tell her that I still haven't **learned to** use chopsticks properly!

Ethel says she needs a few days to get the house ready for your daughter and her friend, so we'd appreciate it if either you or they could give us about a week's notice when they're coming.

Yours,

親愛的艾瑞克：

　　收到您的信，真是個驚喜。

　　就在幾天前，我才向內人艾瑟兒提及，我們應早日寫信給您，恭賀您在聖誕卡片上提到的昇職的事。

　　如信中提及，令嫒計畫到英國來，是嗎？她和朋友若能來家中住個 1、2 天，我們將會非常高興。若令嫒她們二人，不介意同房的話，她們可住二樓湯姆的房間。若二人希望住不同的房間，我們也可把摺疊床搬到三樓的空房。

　　您問我是否還記得梁女士？我當然還記得！她是個如此親切友善的人。當我參觀貴公司的工廠時，受到她很多的照顧。請代我向她致上最衷心的問候，並告訴她，我還是沒能學會如何拿好筷子！

　　艾瑟兒說她需要幾天的時間，為令嫒和她的朋友準備房間。所以若您或她們能在一個禮拜前告訴我們何時抵達的話，我們將不勝感激。

　　　　　　　　　　　　　　　　　　　　　　　　　　　　謹上

【語句注釋】◆ be thrilled 「非常興奮，大為歡喜」。◆ have her come and stay 「她來到並停留」。◆ share 「共用，一起使用」。◆ a camp bed （英式用法）「摺疊床 = cot)」。◆ a spare room （英式用法）「預備的客房」。◆ learn (how) to ～ 「學會～的使用方法」。

【注意】在英國，「一樓」為 ground floor，first floor 則相當於「二樓」，須注意。

原本預定近期訪美，與情同朋友的客戶見面，並約定一起打場高爾夫球，但不得已必須取消約定的書信。

Dear Mr. Simpson,

I have been **looking forward** so much **to meeting** you again in Florida next month, and playing a round of golf with you at the Cypress Park Country Club. Unfortunately a number of **complications** have arisen with the registration of the Forest Junction product name, and I **thought it best to put off** my visit to the States until at least sometime next year.

My legal advisor tells me that, **all being well**, the problem with the registration **should be cleared up** by the end of December, though there is a small possibility that it may **drag on** a little longer.

Whatever happens, it now looks highly unlikely that we shall be able to meet this year. How will you be spending Christmas? Will you be returning to Vermont with your family, or will you be staying in Florida until after the holiday season?

Please give my best regards to your wife Diana, and tell your daughter Jennifer that **Uncle Tom** has not forgotten her, and will send her a small **surprise** for Christmas.

Yours,

辛普森先生台鑒：

　　原本期待下個月在佛羅里達與您見面，並和您在塞普瑞斯鄉村俱樂部打一場高爾夫球，然很遺憾地因 Forest Junction 的商標登錄麻煩不斷，所以我想只得將拜訪美國的計畫，至少延到明年了。

　　我的法律顧問說，事情順利進行的話，商標登錄的問題應可望在 12 月底前解決，不過這件案子仍有延宕的可能性。

　　不管如何，今年我們幾乎是不可能見面了。您將如何度過聖誕節呢？是回到佛蒙特州與家人團聚呢？還是繼續留在佛羅里達州過節呢？

　　請代我向夫人黛安娜致上最誠摯的問候，並告訴令嬡珍妮佛，臺灣的湯姆叔叔並沒有忘記她，而且會寄給她一份聖誕禮物。

　　　　　　　　　　　　　　　　　　　　　　　　　　　　　謹上

語句注釋】◆ **look forward to meeting** 「期待會面」。look forward to 之後須接名詞性的用語。雖也有人使用 look forward to meet，但最好避免此種用法。◆ **complications** 「複雜的狀況；問題的成因」。◆ **I thought it best to put off～** 「我認為最好將～延期」。此時的 think 為不完全及物動詞，it 為受詞，best 則為受詞補語。另一種是，it 為形式上的受詞，真正的受詞為 to put off。I thought it is best to ～ 雖表相同意義，但前者解釋方式在英語中較為普遍。put off 和 postpone 意思相同。◆ **all being well** 「凡事進行順利的話」。此分詞片語，指 if all (things) are (go) well 之意。◆ **should be cleared up** 「應可望解決」。在此 should 為「應可望～」的意思。clear up 和 settle 此時用法大致相同。◆ **drag on** 「拖延」。◆ **Whatever happens** 「不管發生什麼，無論如何」。No matter what happens 或 No matter what may happen 大體上用法皆相同。◆ **Uncle Tom** 「湯姆叔叔」。我們對「父母的兄弟」之外的人，為表示親密而稱為「叔叔」的例子。在英國用法也相同。◆ **surprise** 「驚喜的禮物」。

6

致歉信函

6-1　取消約定的致歉函

　　本約定見面，然因飛機班次預約的錯誤，故無法在約定的時間碰面。除了道歉之外，同時，希望約定下次見面的一封信。

Dear Mr. Nishimura,

I am extremely sorry for the inconvenience my abrupt can cellation of our June 16 meeting must have caused you.

As I told your secretary over the phone, it was not until I arrived at Fukuoka Airport that I noticed the mistake my travel agent had made in my plane reservation. I tried to change to another flight, but found that all flights by all carriers were fully booked for the next four hours. I had no option but to call your office and cancel our meeting.

My next visit to Tokyo will be on June 27, and I hope to be in town for at least three days. I would appreciate an opportunity to meet with you at that time.

Please let me know the most convenient time and day for you.

Sincerely yours,

西村先生台鑒：

　　本人對於臨時取消 6 月 16 日的會面對您所造成的不便，深深感到抱歉。

　　如同我在電話中告訴您的祕書的，直到我到了福岡機場，才發現旅行社訂錯了班機。雖試著更換其他班機，卻被告知近 4 小時內的各航空公司的班機都已全部客滿。在別無選擇的情況下，我只得打電話到貴辦公室取消約定。

　　我下一次拜訪東京的時間是 6 月 27 日，希望至少能停留 3 天。屆時，若有機會與您見面，將不勝感激。

　　請告知您最方便的時間與日期。

謹上

語句注釋】◆ **inconvenience**　「不便，困擾」。因 trouble 語氣稍嫌誇張，故在一般場合多半使用 inconvenience。◆ **abrupt**　「意外的，突然的」。◆ **over the phone**　「以電話～」。也可說為 on the phone 或 by telephone。◆ **it was not until … that ～**　「一直到…才～」。◆ **book**　「預約」。與 reserve 相同。◆ **I had no option but ～**　「除了～之外無選擇餘地；除了～之外別無其他選擇」。在此 but 為表「除了～之外」的關係代名詞。option 則為「選擇的自由」之意。與 I had no choice but ～ 大致上相同。◆ **I hope to be in town**　「希望停留在（東京）」。與 I think (expect) I will be in town 大致上相同，hope 表示寄予希望地預測。因在此刻還只是個約定，故不說 I will be in town，給予些許緩衝空間的表現。in town 為「在市區（東京）」之意。◆ **meet with you**　「與閣下會面」。約定會面時，不用 meet you，一般為 meet with you。

6-2 對自己擅自介紹對方的致歉函

為自己在談話過程中擅自提及對方姓名，因而使對方受到工作邀約一事致歉，並說明對方在抉擇時，不須顧慮自己，即使拒絕邀約也沒關係的一封信。

Dear Tom:

I sincerely hope that an inappropriate comment I made last week hasn't put you in a difficult position.

I was having lunch with Takashi Ueda, the president of Fujitec, and one or two other senior executives. As I'm sure you know, Takashi is a great connoisseur of art, and has an exceptionally fine collection of prints and paintings from all over the world.

We got to talking about modern American artists, and I mentioned that you and I had gone to the same high school together, and that we were still good friends. Takashi became very excited about this, and immediately suggested that I contact you and ask you to design a new logo mark for our company.

I feel a little bad about this. I would hate to think you felt under any obligation to accept just because the initial approach came from me.

Please let me know in all honesty what you think about this proposal. I will not be in the least offended if you decline, and neither will Takashi.

Yours,

親愛的湯姆：

　　由衷地希望我在上個禮拜的不當舉動，沒有為您帶來任何困擾。

　　當時我和富士科技公司總裁上田隆先生，及另外兩位高級主管共進午餐。相信你一定知道，總裁是位藝術品的優秀行家，並收藏有各地珍貴版畫及油畫。

　　當話題談到有關現代美國畫家時，我無意中提到了我曾和您上過同一高中，目前仍是好朋友一事。總裁得知此事後即雀躍地建議我與您聯絡，並請您為本公司設計一全新的商標。

　　我為此感到抱歉。若您因為最初與您洽談的人是我，而覺得有接受的義務，我將為此感到非常的難過。

　　請坦白地告訴我您對此邀約的想法。即使您無意接受而拒絕，我和總裁也不會因此而感到不悅。

敬上

【語句注釋】◆ put you in a difficult position 「將您置於棘手的立場」。◆ senior executive 「高級主管」。◆ connoisseur 「鑑賞家，行家」。◆ print 「版畫；(美術品的)複製」。在此應指版畫。◆ get to talking 「開始說到～，言及～」。◆ become excited about ～ 「對～感到非常有興趣」。◆ logo mark 「商標」。◆ feel bad about～ 「對～感到遺憾」。這裡的用法與 feel sorry about ～的說法大致相同。◆ hate to think 「根本不想～」。◆ feel under obligation 「認為自己有義務，感到有義務」。◆ initial approach 「最初的推動，發起，媒介」。◆ in all honesty 「完全正直地，不隱藏地，無忌憚地」。◆ I will not be in the least offended 「我完全不在意」。not in the least 指「一點也不～」之意。offend 指「傷及感情，使不悅」的意思。◆ decline 「拒絕」。因 reject 和 refuse 口氣太過強硬，通常使用 decline。◆ neither will Takashi 「Takashi 也不會～」。為 Takashi will not be offended either.「Takashi 也不會因～感到介意(不愉快)」的簡化用法。

6-3 對訴怨信函的致歉函

　　顧客服務部轉給業務部，新近購買了洗碗機的顧客對售後服務有所不滿的訴怨信函。業務部通知當事人，下星期將協同維修工程師一同到府拜訪，直接協助處理的一封信。

Dear Mrs. Merivale,

Our Customer Relations Department has passed on to me your letter of March 23, in which you describe some of the difficulties you have had with obtaining satisfactory service for your new dishwasher.

On behalf of Starline, may I offer you our unconditional apologies for any inconvenience you have experienced.

If I may, I should like to accompany our engineer when he calls on you next Thursday, and discuss with you in person the problems you have been having.

Yours faithfully,

梅莉華女士台鑒：

　　本公司之顧客服務部已將您 3 月 23 日的來信轉交給我。來信中，您描述到幾點因對新購買的洗碗機未得到令人滿意的服務，而感到困擾的地方。

　　在此謹代表星條公司，對您所遭受到的不便之處，深表萬分歉意。

　　若您方便的話，下個星期四我將協同本公司之工程師同行，登門拜訪，直接聽取您目前所面臨的問題。

　　　　　　　　　　　　　　　　　　　　　　　　　　　　謹上

【語句注釋】◆ **Customer Relations Department**　「顧客服務部」。◆ **pass on to ～** 「轉送」之意，故也可使用 forward, transfer 等。◆ **on behalf of ～**　「謹代表～」。◆ **unconditional apologies**　「無條件的道歉，深感抱歉」。an unconditional surrender 則為 「無條件投降」。◆ **If I may (accompany)**　「若可以的話，我將（協同～一起拜訪）」。◆ **accompany**　「同行」。◆ **discuss with you in person**　「直接與對方討論」。in person「本人直接」。

【注意】自古以來就有著，業務人員若能妥善的處理訴怨，即可獨當一面的說法。由此也可看出，訴怨信函的處理對於業務人員是多麼的重要。從顧客方面收到任何表示不滿的信件時，即使感到「不合理」，重要的是，首先須採取低姿態。其次，表示自己有解決問題的誠意。

因內部的聯繫不周，致使讓已約好時間見面的對方久等的致歉信函。

Dear Mr. Moore,

It has been brought to my notice that you were kept waiting for over one hour when you visited our Akasaka Office on Monday, September 5. Please accept my sincerest apologies for the completely unacceptable treatment you received on that day.

I have spoken to both the receptionist on duty at the time you called, and to Mr. Yoshioka, the person with whom you had a 10:00 am appointment. Please allow me to offer an explanation of what happened.

Our receptionist confirms that you visited our office at 9:55 am, and that she immediately put through a call to our Advertising Department to announce your arrival. Mr. Yoshioka had still not arrived in his office at that time, and that is why you were asked to wait in the lobby of our building.

When Mr. Yoshioka did arrive in his office at approximately 10:15 am, he was not informed that you were waiting in the lobby, and assumed that you were late for your appointment. It was not until well after 11:00 am that the receptionist called the Advertising Department again to point out that you were still waiting.

In addition to speaking with everyone involved, I have taken steps to ensure that this kind of thing does not happen again.

If at all possible, I should like to visit your office at your convenience, and offer my apologies to you in person.

Yours sincerely,

莫爾先生台鑒:

　　獲報知悉閣下於 9 月 5 日星期一，來訪本公司赤坂辦事處時，空等了 1 個小時以上一事。在此為您當日所受到之不當待遇，真誠地致上歉意。

　　本人已和當時您拜訪本事務所時，負責接待的人員以及與您約定於上午 10 點會面的吉岡先生兩人照會過。容我在此就當日所發生的情況，加以說明解釋。

　　本事務所的接待員確定了您於上午 9 點 55 分蒞臨本公司後，隨即以電話向宣傳部通告您的到來。然而當時因吉岡先生尚未進辦公室，因此請您在大廳中稍候。

　　當吉岡於上午 10 點 15 分左右到達公司時，並沒有人告訴他您在大廳中等候的消息，於是，吉岡以為您遲到。直到過了 11 點之後，接待員才再度以電話通知宣傳部門，您一直在大廳等候一事。

　　我除了提醒相關人員注意之外，並進一步地確認今後不會再發生類似的情況。

　　若可能的話，我希望在您方便的時間，造訪貴公司，親自致上我的歉意。

謹上

【語句注釋】◆ **It has been brought to my notice that** ～ 「我注意到～，～傳到我耳中」。bring ～ to a person's notice「～引起某人的注意」之意。It 為形式上的主詞，真主詞為 that 之後的子句。notice 之外，attention 也具有相同的意思。◆ **keep ～ waiting**「讓～久等」。I'm sorry to have kept you waiting.（很抱歉讓您久等。）的句子經常為人使用。◆ **over one hour**「1 個小時以上」。在此 over 指 more than 之意。◆ **completely unacceptable treatment**「完全地無法令人接受的待遇」。◆ **speak to ～**「和～談話」。有時含有「忠告；斥責」的意思。◆ **on duty**「值勤，勤務中」。相反則為 off duty（下班）。◆ **a 10:00 am appointment**「上午 10 點的約定」。a.m. 或 p.m. 為美式用法。英國普遍如 am 和 pm 所示，不加縮寫點。此外，一般 am 和 pm 附加於時間之後，a.m. 10:00 或 p.m. 3:30 則為錯誤的寫法。「約定會面」為 appointment 而不是 promise。本來 I made a promise with him to meet at 10:00 am. 的說法在文法上並無錯誤，但通常說成 I have an appointment with him for 10:00 am.。◆ **put through a call to ～**「打電話給～；以電話聯絡～」。◆ **When Mr. Yoshioka did arrive in his office**「當吉岡來到辦公室時」。英語中，對他公司的人提及自己公司的人時，加上 Mr.／Mrs.／Miss／Ms. 等敬稱，並不感覺奇怪。did arrive 為強調 arrived 的用法。含有「確實（總算）抵達」的語氣在內。◆ **arrive in his office**「到達他的辦公室」。介系詞為 in 時，讓人有一種到達寬廣的辦公室之中的感覺。若使用 at，則予人到達辦公室此一地點的感覺。◆ **It was not until well after 11:00 that ～**「一直到過了 11 點才～」。（請參照範例 6–1 的【語句注釋】）。◆ **point out**「指摘，指出」。◆ **If at all possible**「可能的話」。at all 含有「恐怕不行」的語氣。完整句子為 If it is at all possible，it 指「拜訪貴公司」。◆ **in person**「親自；本人」。

回覆範例 6–4 的善意回信。請對方對於自己前些日子拜訪該公司時，因接待人員聯絡的疏失，而在大廳久候一事，無需在意。

Dear Mr. Abe,

Many thanks for your letter of September 8. I appreciate your taking the time to **look into** the small misunderstanding that occurred when I visited your company last week.

Please rest assured that an apology was neither necessary or expected. These kinds of things happen all the time, even in the best-organized companies, and **I wouldn't be surprised if** visitors are sometimes kept waiting in our office for an hour or more.

You say that you would like to come and offer your apologies **in person**. This is really not necessary, but you are, of course, welcome to come and visit our company **at any time**.

I am usually in my office most of the day, but a phone call **ahead of time** would be appreciated.

Yours sincerely,

阿部先生台鑒：

　　謝謝您於 9 月 8 日的來信。並對本人於上週拜訪貴公司時發生的小誤會，特撥出時間進行了解一事深表感激。

　　請不要將此事掛在心上，因為既無道歉之必要，我本人也不期待。像此類的事情，即使是在最有組織的公司，也經常發生；若有訪客在我們公司等上 1 個多小時的事情發生，我也不會因而感到驚愕。

　　您提及您有意到本公司親自致歉一事，我認為並無此必要。不過，若您堅持來訪，當然，我們隨時都歡迎您大駕光臨。

　　我平常幾乎整天都在辦公室，不過若能事先來電告知，將不勝感激。

謹上

【語句注釋】◆ look into 「調查」。investigate 的委婉表現。◆ Please rest assured that ～ 「因為～故請安心」。直譯則為「使～確定；確定～」。也可說 Please be assured ～.◆ I wouldn't be surprised if ～ 「若～我也不驚訝」。「不稀奇」之意。在此 if 為 even if（即使～也）的意思。◆ in person 「親自」。與 personally 相同。◆ at any time 「無論何時」。◆ ahead of time 「事前」。其意義與 in advance 或 beforehand 類似。

7

請求委託信函

7-1 委託翻譯

目前委任的口譯人員似乎無法確切地傳達談話中的弦外之音，因此請求對方擔任此次口譯人員的一封信。

Dear Mr. Funada,

I shall be in Tokyo next month, and on November 12 I am scheduled to meet with Jun Uematsu of Trans-Ocean to discuss a problem that has come up with regard to our contract arrangement.

It promises to be a rather difficult meeting, and I want to make sure that there are no communication difficulties or misunderstandings. For this reason I would prefer not to use my regular interpreter, Miss Eguchi. Although I have found her very efficient and professional in the past, what I really need this time is someone who can "read" the negotiating position of both parties in the discussion, and can interpret accordingly.

I know that you are an extremely busy man ,and I feel a little bad about asking you to help me out in this way, but could you possibly set aside an hour or two on November 12?

My meeting with Jun Uematsu is scheduled for 2:00 pm, but if some other time is more convenient for you, I think I can persuade him to change the timing.

Yours faithfully,

船田先生大鑒：

　　我將於下個月到東京，並定於 11 月 12 日與大洋運輸公司的植松潤先生會面，商討有關契約合同所產生的一些問題。

　　此次會談想必將相當困難，而且我希望能確認彼此之間沒有任何溝通上的困難或誤解。因此緣故，此回我不打算用我的常任口譯員江口小姐。雖然我從過去的經驗中，知道她很有才能並且非常專業，但是此回我所真正需要的，是個在會議的場合中，能夠「讀取」交涉中雙方的立場，且能為之「傳譯」的人。

　　我知道您非常的忙碌，並覺得自己提出如此希望協助的請求，著實有些不妥。但不知是否可能在 11 月 12 日，撥出 1、2 個小時呢？

　　我和植松潤先生的會談定於下午 2 點，不過若其他時間對您較為方便，我想我應可說服對方更改時間。

謹上

【語句注釋】◆ **be scheduled to ～** 「預定（做）～」。◆ **with regard to** 「關於」。
◆ **promise to be** 「預料將有～的可能」。He promise to be a great musician.（預料他將成為偉大的音樂家）。◆ **I want to make sure that ～** 「我想確認～」。◆ **I would prefer not to ～** 「我傾向於不要～」。◆ **someone who can "read" ～** 「能『讀取』（察知）～的」。◆ **accordingly** 「適當地，相應地」。◆ **set aside** 「抽出（時間）」。
◆ **persuade him to ～** 「說服他做～」。

　　自己雖非專業的口譯人員，但很高興能為老朋友幫上忙。因在正式會談之前，事先得有些了解，故希望對方能寄來到目前為止經過情形的資料。此外，在談及工作之餘，亦邀約一起用餐敘舊的信。

Dear Mr. Yardley,

Thank you for your letter of October 23. I was delighted to hear that you will be in Tokyo again, and that we'll have an opportunity to see each other again.

As you say, **my work keeps me very busy**, and I don't really consider myself an interpreter, but I shall **be only too pleased** to set aside time for an old friend like yourself, and help in any way I can.

Two o'clock **on the afternoon of November 12** is fine with me, **as long as** the **venue** is not too far from my office in Nihonbashi.

It would help me a lot if you could send me copies of any previous correspondence relating to the subject matter of your discussion with Mr. Uematsu. It will give me some idea of the **developments** so far.

By the way, how long will you be in Japan this time? It would be nice if **we** could also **get together** a little more **informally**—dinner at my favorite sushi restaurant, perhaps, or a few drinks at the British pub in Ebisu.

Yours,

雅德里先生大鑒：

　　謝謝您 10 月 23 日的來信。很高興得知您將再度來到東京，我們彼此能有機會再見面。

　　正如您所說，工作令我相當忙碌，而且我也不認為自己稱得上口譯人員。不過，我很高興自己能撥出時間，為了如您一般的老友幫上一點忙。

　　若會議的場所，離我在日本橋附近的辦公室不遠的話，11 月 12 日的下午 2 點，應沒有什麼問題。

　　若您能寄來，到目前為止，您和植松先生之間有關於此事的往來書信的影本，將大為助益。因為我想如此應能對直至目前的來龍去脈，有所了解。

　　對了，此回您將在日本停留多久呢？若我們能聚在一起，放鬆一下該有多好。——比方說，到我最喜歡的壽司店用餐，或者，到惠比壽的英式酒吧喝幾杯。

　　　　　　　　　　　　　　　　　　　　　　　　謹上

【語句注釋】◆ my work keeps me very busy 「工作令我相當忙碌」。keep＋（人、物）＋形容詞、副詞、介系詞的句型，為「將（人、物）保持在某個狀態、動作、位置」的意思。例如：keep (a person) informed（與某人不間斷地聯繫）、keep (a person) away from ~（使某人遠離~）。◆ be only too pleased 「非常的高興」。◆ on the afternoon of November 12 「在 11 月 12 日下午」。通常為 in the afternoon，不過當後面限定於某日期時，介系詞 in 則變為 on。◆ as long as ~ 「只要~」。◆ venue 「會場」。本為法律用語，此處指會談的場所。◆ developments 「（事態的）進展，新情況」。◆ we get together informally 「（放下工作等）輕鬆地聚在一起」。

為了決定應徵者的錄用與否，將舉行英語的面試，詢問對方是否能為之擔任面試官的書信。

Dear Mr. Davidson,

On July 13-15 we shall be holding interviews at our **head office** in Kaohsiung for approximately two hundred **job applicants**.

We are anxious that successful applicants have a **firm command of English**, so this year, in addition to the usual interviews given by members of our **personnel department**, we should like to give the applicants a short interview in English.

At the moment we **envisage** interviewing three applicants at a time, and limiting each interview to about ten minutes.

If you are available on any of the above three days, we should like to ask you to take part in the interviews, and are prepared to offer a **remuneration** of five hundred yen per interview, plus travel expenses.

Please let me know if these conditions are acceptable to you, and on which days you are available.

Yours sincerely,

戴維森先生台鑒：

　　本公司將於 7 月 13 日～15 日，對約 200 名的求職者，在本公司的高雄總公司舉行面試。

　　我們期望合格者須具有相當的英語能力，因此今年除了將在人事部舉行一般性的面試之外，也希望加上以英文進行的簡短面試。

　　目前，我們考慮一次同時面試三位應徵者，面試時間限制在約 10 分鐘以內。

　　若您在上述的 3 日中的任何一天方便的話，我們希望麻煩您為我們擔任面試官。報酬方面，每次的面試為 500 日圓，車馬費另計。

　　若您能接受上述的條件，請通知我們，並告訴我們您方便的日子。

謹上

【語句注釋】◆ head office　「總公司」。也可說成 main office 或 headquarters。◆ job applicant　「應徵者」。指求職者 (job seeker) 中已提出申請 (application) 的人。◆ firm command of English　「具有相當的英文能力」。在此，command 為「自由運用的能力」之意。◆ personnel department　「人事部門」。不要與 personal（個人的）混淆。◆ envisage　「預想，推測」。如 envisage interviewing 所示，envisage 的後面接動名詞，不接不定詞，須注意!◆ remuneration　「報酬」。

對於委託擔任英語面試官的請託，傳達自己在時間上允許的同時，對於報酬以及面試方式提出自己的希望的一封信。

Dear Mr. Wood,

Many thanks for your letter of June 30.

I am free on all of the three days you have scheduled for your interviews. The **remuneration** you offer (500 yen per interview) is, however, **considerably** lower than I would normally accept.

I am fairly flexible **when it comes to** negotiating rates for conversation classes, seminars, speech contest judging, etc. If your company is **considering making** English interviews an **integral** part of its selection process, and if I could **be assured of** similar work in the future, I would be prepared to accept 600 yen per interview this year, **on the understanding that** you would be prepared to offer a little more next year.

With regard to the interviews themselves, I am not too happy about **tackling** three applicants at one time. I strongly **suggest that you consider arranging** individual interviews, even if this means **extensive rescheduling**.

Yours sincerely,

伍德先生台鑒：

　　謝謝您於 6 月 30 日的來信。

　　貴公司預定面試的三天期間，我並沒有其他預定。不過，對於您所提供的一次面試 500 日圓的酬勞，實在比我通常所能接受的為低。

　　在商議英語會話課程、研習會、演講比賽的裁判等的酬勞時，我通常相當有彈性。若貴公司計畫將此類英語面試作為選擇應徵者的過程中的要項，並能確保今後也將提供本人類似的工作的話，我能夠接受今年度一次面試 600 日圓的酬勞，不過必須是在明年度以後，再提高些許之下為前提。

　　至於有關面試本身，我不太希望一次同時面試三個人。我極力建議，即使貴公司須作大幅度地計畫變更，也最好安排個人單一的面試。

謹上

【語句注釋】◆ remuneration 「報酬，酬勞」。◆ considerably 「相當的」。比 much 保守含蓄的說法，但比 fairly 的程度還多的感覺。◆ when it comes to ＋名詞 「當談及～」。◆ consider ～ing 「考慮做～」。consider 之後接動名詞，不接不定詞，consider to do 為錯誤的用法，須注意!◆ integral 「必須的」。◆ be assured of～ 「得到～的保證」。assure（人）of（事、物）＝向（某人）保證（某事、某物）。◆ on the understanding that ～ 「在了解到～的情況下」。◆ tackle 「阻截；擒抱並摔倒對方球員」。◆ suggest that you consider ～ing 「提議貴公司考慮～」。有如 suggest, recommend, advise, request, urge 等，在表示提議、請託、要求等的主要子句後接續的附屬子句中，注意使用動詞的原形。也可說～ that you should consider。◆ extensive rescheduling 「大幅地更改預定計畫」。

回應範例 7–4 中，負責面試的預定人選所提出的要求，雖然此回可將一次面試的酬勞提高到 600 日圓，但未能確定來年是否能提供相同的工作機會的一封信。

Dear Mr. Davidson,

I have spoken with the head of our **accounting section**, and she has **agreed to our offering** you a revised remuneration of six hundred yen per interview.

I cannot, unfortunately, offer you any guarantee of **similar work** next year. Please understand that this is the first time we have included English interviews in our personnel selection process, and we **intend making** a decision about next year only after reviewing what happens in July.

I fully understand your **reservations** about interviewing three applicants at one time. Individual interviews are, however, impractical because of the number of applicants we have to process, and the limited time available.

If you are still prepared to help us with the interviews, please let me know as soon as possible.

Yours sincerely,

戴維森先生台鑒：

　　我與本公司的會計課課長商談的結果，她同意將酬勞更改為一次面試 600 日圓。

　　不過很遺憾的，我並不能向您保證明年度類似的工作。並請了解，此回為本公司首次決定將英語的面試納入人事徵選的過程，我們只能在檢討今年 7 月施行的結果後，方能為明年度作決定。

　　我十分理解您對同時面試三名應徵者的作法的顧念，但就所必須處理的應徵者人數以及時間上的限制來考量，個人面試是無法實行的。

　　若您能接納上述的條件，協助此回的面試，請儘早地通知我們。

　　　　　　　　　　　　　　　　　　　　　　　　　　　謹上

因為公司駐外人員的簽證不久即將到期，需要重新申請，並且從駐外人員的聯絡得知，必須請持有當地國籍的人為駐外人員擔保才行。因為在當地除了對方以外，沒有其他人可提供協助，請無論如何務必幫忙的請求信。

Dear Mr. Kowalski,

Mr. Ken'ichi Yamatake, our representative in Warsaw, has written to tell us that his visa status has been queried, and that he must reapply for a new visa if he wishes to continue living and working in Poland.

Our head office is at the moment preparing the documents necessary for this application. He has, however, been informed that he will also have to submit a reference from a Polish national.

I am writing to ask you if you would kindly furnish him with this reference. It is my understanding that this is something of a formality, and serves only to confirm the identity of the applicant.

I must apologize for making such a request of you, but I can think of no better person to ask.

Yours sincerely,

克渥斯基先生台鑒：

　　本公司的駐華沙辦事處代表山武健一來信告訴我們，他目前所持
簽證的狀況受到審查。因此若希望繼續留在波蘭工作的話，他必須重
新申請新的簽證。

　　本公司目前正為其準備申請所需的各項證件，不過，他被告知必
須提出持有波蘭國籍的人士所作的人身保證書。

　　謹以此信詢問您可否為他提供保證書？據我所知，此保證書不過
是形式上的手續，只用以確認申請者的身分。

　　在此為提出如是請求，深感歉意。實乃因為除您之外，沒有其他
合適的人可以懇託。

　　　　　　　　　　　　　　　　　　　　　　　　　　　　謹上

語句注釋】◆ visa status　「簽證情況」。◆ query　「審問，查詢」。◆ at the
moment　「現在，目前」。◆ reference　「人身保證書，信用保證函」。◆ a Polish
national　「持有波蘭國籍的人」。◆ something of a formality　「形式上的（東西）」。
mething of the kind [or sort]　（諸如此類的東西）。◆ serve only to ～　「只用於～」。
◆ confirm the identity　「確認身分」。◆ make such a request of you　「向您提出如
的請求」。◆ think of ～　「想到，想起～」。

7-6　委託擔任簽證申請之必要保證人的請求　117

7-7 請求協助募款

　　為了身體殘障的日本兒童，希望設立一法律上認可的基金會。而成立基金會，必須存入一億日圓的保證金，現在正推行募款活動中，懇請對方贊助協力募款的請求信。

Dear Sir:

The Sunrise Association, founded in 1972, is a nationwide **voluntary organization** providing support for physically and mentally **challenged children** here in Japan. We hope the enclosed materials will give some idea of the nature and scope of our activities.

We take this opportunity to write to you **in connection with** our **efforts to raise** the **money** necessary to change the status of our Association to that of a legally recognized **foundation**.

At present in Japan, only officially registered foundations are allowed to receive financial assistance and **welfare grants**. To acquire the status of a foundation, however, requires the deposit of a guaranty of one hundred million Japanese yen.

We respectfully ask for any financial assistance you may be able to afford our Association in the **raising** of the one million dollars we need to continue our work for challenged children.

The thousand folded-paper cranes we enclose were made by lady volunteers and **well-wishers**, and are a traditional Japanese way of expressing a sincere and **fervent** desire for the fulfillment of a hope or wish.

Sincerely,

敬啟者：

　　「朝陽協會」創立於 1972 年，乃一為了幫助在身體上以及智能上有障礙的日本兒童的全國性義工組織。我們希望信中所附之資料，將給您一些對於我們的本質及活動內容大體上的概念。

　　我們藉此機會致信與您，乃是為了籌募將我們的協會變更為法律上認可的基金會所需之儲備金的募款活動。

　　日本在目前只有官方認可的基金會，才能獲得財政上的補助以及社會福利津貼。然而，為了取得基金會的身分，必須支付一億日圓的保證金。

　　我們懇請您提供任何您能提供的財力援助，幫助本協會籌募為了繼續支援身心障礙的兒童所須的一百萬美金。

　　隨函附上的千羽鶴，乃由婦女義工朋友們及支持此活動的人士所摺成。是日本人傳統上祈求希望、願望達成時，表現衷心與熱誠的一種方式。

謹上

【語句注釋】◆ voluntary organization 「義務性的組織」。◆ challenged children 「身心障礙的兒童」。比 disabled children「殘障兒童」更為委婉的表現。◆ in connection with ～ 「與～相關 (= in regard to)」。◆ efforts to raise money 「募款活動」。efforts 一字在英國也有「募款活動」的意思。◆ foundation 「基金會，社會事業團體」。association 指「協會，團體，工會」等，與法律上認可、公開登錄註冊的 foundation 不同。◆ welfare grant 「福利補助金，援助金」。◆ raise 「籌募（資金等）」。◆ well-wisher 「（～主義等的）支持者」。◆ fervent 「有熱誠的」。

　　本基金會乃為了紀念公司的創立者而設立的，所以資金來源也很有限。很抱歉無法響應貴協會的援助要求為主旨的拒絕信函。

Dear Ms. Kotani:

Many thanks for your letter and the **descriptive material** about the wonderful work your Association is doing for physically and mentally challenged children in Taiwan. Many thanks also for the beautiful paper cranes created by your **devoted** volunteers.

As you are no doubt **aware**, the Koniger Foundation, created **in memory of** the founder of our company, exists to provide financial help and support to **charitable institutions** such as yours. Our resources are, however, limited, and we are not able to respond to all of the many requests we receive.

Grants for the next three years have already been assigned, and I am sorry to say that we **are not in a position to** assist your efforts to change the status of your Association.

May I wish you all success in your **worthy cause**, and **thank you for your interest in** our Foundation.

Sincerely,

小谷小姐台鑒：

　　多謝您的來信以及詳述有關貴協會為了身心障礙的日本兒童所作的各項傑出的活動資料。也很感謝服務奉獻的義工們所摺的美麗紙鶴。

　　相信您也知道，柯尼格基金會乃為了紀念本公司的創立者而設立，旨在於提供有如貴協會等的慈善團體，財力上的支持與援助。然而，我們的財源也很有限。因此，我們無法完全回應所有希望我們援助的許多請求。

　　今後 3 年內的援助金配置已經決定。很遺憾地在此告知您，我們無法對貴協會資格變更的募款活動加以援助。

　　在此祈祝貴協會令人敬佩的募款活動得以順利成功，並感謝您對本基金會所抱持的關心。

謹上

【語句注釋】◆ descriptive material 「說明性的資料」。◆ devoted 「奉獻的，獻身性的」。◆ as you are aware 「如您所知」。◆ in memory of ～ 「紀念～」。◆ charitable institutions 「慈善團體」。◆ be not in a position to ～ 「不能夠～」。因 cannot 更為委婉，故多使用於書信中。◆ worthy cause 「可敬的、有意義的活動」。cause 本為「（社會運動中的）理想，目標，主義」等意思，不過在此指為了如此目標所進的「活動」。◆ thank you for your interest in ～ 「謝謝您對～所抱持的關心」。為無回應對方的請託要求時，經常使用的說法。

為了籌集募款的慈善義賣會暨烤肉大會所需的摸彩獎品，向當地的各公司團體請求贊助的一封信。

Dear Sir:

On Saturday, June 16 the Brompton High School for Girls will be holding its annual **fund-raising** Bazaar and Barbecue, and as usual the PTA is asking local companies to help by **contributing prizes** to the Lucky Prize **Draw**, or by **taking advertising space** in the Bazaar and Barbecue program.

Each year, companies such as yours have helped to make the Bazaar and Barbecue **a resounding success**, and I am sure you will wish to join them in supporting one of the most important events in our school year.

I am enclosing a copy of our program for last year, and on Page 48 you will find a list of the prizes offered in last year's Lucky Prize Draw. As you can see, the names of the contributing companies are **featured prominently**, providing some excellent public relations. Furthermore, the names of the companies contributing the top three prizes are also featured on all the Lucky Prize Draw tickets.

Please let me know as soon as possible if you are interested in supporting one of the oldest and most **prestigious** schools in Brompton.

Yours truly,

敬啟者:

　　6 月 16 日星期六將於布朗普敦女子高中舉行一年一度的募款慈善義賣暨烤肉大會。依照慣例,本家長會希望本地的公司,能協助提供幸運抽獎活動的獎品或在義賣會節目表上刊登廣告。

　　每一年在如貴公司的公司團體熱心援助下,使得歷屆的慈善義賣暨烤肉大會得以圓滿且成功。深信貴公司也願意加入支援本校最重要的年度行事之一的義賣年會的行列。

　　隨函附上去年的節目表一份。其中第 48 頁刊登有去年的幸運抽獎活動中所有獎品一覽表。如您所見,各贊助公司的大名皆清楚顯目的刊登於其上,為相當傑出的宣傳廣告。而且,贊助前三項大獎的公司名字,也將被印在所有的摸彩券上。

　　若您有意贊助布朗普敦歷史最悠久,也最具名望的學校之一的本校,請即速與我們聯絡。

　　　　　　　　　　　　　　　　　　　　　　　　　　謹呈

【語句注釋】◆ **fund-raising** 「募款」。◆ **contribute prizes** 「贊助提供獎品」。◆ **draw** 「抽獎」。take a draw in a lottery(摸彩)。◆ **take advertising space** 「刊登廣告」。◆ **a resounding success** 「圓滿成功」。resounding「完全地,徹底地」。a resounding popular success(深受歡迎的成功。)◆ **feature** 「(報紙等上)大大地刊登」。◆ **prominently** 「突顯地,顯眼地」。◆ **prestigious** 「深具名望的」。a prestige school「名校」。

關於獎品的贊助，已由公司經理正式批准。此外，經理對於在節目表中可刊登公司廣告一事也相當有興趣，並已指示廣告的負責人，將針對詳細情形與其聯絡。

Dear Mrs. Howe,

I have shown your letter and program to Mr. Liang, our area manager, and I am pleased to tell you that he has authorized the donation of one of our latest 29-inch AV model television sets to your Lucky Prize Draw.

Please let me know where and when you would like us to ship this item to you, and I will make the necessary arrangements with one of our local distributors.

Mr. Liang has also expressed an interest in placing an advertisement in your Bazaar and Barbecue program, and has instructed Ms. Lynch, our PR manager, to contact you directly and discuss the details.

Sincerely,

霍爾女士雅鑒：

　　在呈上您的來信及節目表給本公司的區域經理梁先生之後，很榮幸的在此通知您，他已批准同意提供本公司最新型的 AV 型 29 吋電視機一臺贊助貴校的抽獎活動。

　　請告知您希望我們將此臺電視機送達的時間和地點，我們將與當地的經銷商做必要的安排。

　　此外，梁經理對於在此次義賣會的節目表上刊載公司廣告一事相當有興趣，並已指示本公司的廣告部經理林區小姐，直接與您聯絡並商討細節。

謹上

【語句注釋】◆ authorize　「正式批准」。◆ make necessary arrangements with ～
銷商」。◆ express an interest in ～　「對～表示關心，對～感興趣」。express 也可以
ow 代替。

【注意】海外經商時，所經銷的產品與消費者的關係越密切，越有必要融入當地，以提高
司的知名度。因此，積極地參與義賣會或烤肉大會等，對當地社會付出貢獻實屬必要。
得的回報可能大上幾十倍，決不會因贊助了一臺電視而吃虧的。此經理的睦鄰決策，絕
可作為讀者諸君的參考。

指導學生們針對「生產」這個主題進行調查研究。雖然也已準備好了參考書籍、錄影帶等資料，但百聞不如一見，於是洽詢在學校附近的一家工廠是否能讓學生們實習參觀的委託信函。

Dear Sir:

Next month my class of fifth graders will be exploring the theme of Production, and among the many topics they will be investigating is the manufacture of everyday household objects.

My assistant Ms. Fletcher and I have prepared a number of stimulating and instructive materials for our students, including books, magazines, and video tapes.

None of these can, however, compare with a visit to a real factory, and we were wondering if it would be at all possible to take our students around your Kingsbury plant, which is only about five miles from our school.

If, for reasons of safety or security, you do not accept such educational tours, we will of course understand fully.

We have to finalize next month's lesson schedule by Thursday of next week, and we would appreciate an answer from you before then.

Sincerely,

敬啟者：

　　我所指導的5年級班級，將於下個月針對「生產」一題進行探究。在他們即將進行調查的諸多主題中，有一項是有關日常家庭用品的製造過程。

　　我的助理佛莉蕎小姐和本人，已為學生們準備了許多深具啟發性且有助學習的教材，包括書籍、雜誌、錄影帶等。

　　然而這些資料都比不上實地的工廠參觀。因此不知是否可以帶我們的學生到距離本校只有5哩遠的貴公司金柏利工廠參觀？

　　若基於安全與機密的理由，貴公司並不接受此類教育性質的參觀，我們當然能夠完全體諒。

　　因我們必須在下星期四之前，對下個月的課程作最後的定案。若貴公司能在這之前給我們答覆，我們將十分感激。

謹上

因為公司對於接待工廠參觀早已做了系統性地規劃，故屆時將竭誠歡迎來訪的回函。

Dear Ms. Silverman:

Your query about a tour of our Kingsbury plant has been forwarded to me for reply, and I am happy to say that we do organize tours of our factory, and would be delighted to show your class of fifth graders around.

You express concern about safety and security. We do not, as a rule, take visitors into areas of the plant that might expose them to the slightest danger. We do ask that children be accompanied by responsible adults, but this will be no problem in your case.

If you could let me know how many children you will be bringing, and what time they will be arriving, I am sure that we can work out a plant tour that will be both interesting and educational.

Could you also let me know if we need to make any special arrangements for members of your party.

Sincerely,

席佛蒙小姐惠鑒:

您詢問有關本公司金柏利工廠的參觀實習的來信,已轉送到我手邊,由本人回覆。在此很榮幸的告知您,我們已對工廠的參觀做了系統性的行程規劃,我們將很樂意帶領貴班 5 年級的學生參觀本廠。

至於您對安全及機密方面的顧慮,原則上,我們不帶領訪客到可能略具輕微危險性的區域參觀。並且,我們通常要求孩童必須由監護的大人陪同。但此點對您的狀況而言,並不會產生問題。

若您能告知,將帶領多少學生和何時抵達的話,我保證我們能籌畫出一個既有趣又富教育性的工廠參觀實習。

此外,若您需要我們為您的學生作任何特別的安排,也請一併告知。

謹上

【語句注釋】◆ show (a person) around 「帶領(人)參觀」。◆ express concern 「關心,表示掛念」。◆ as a rule 「原則上」。也表「一般,大概」的意思。◆ expose (a person) to ～ 「使(人)暴露於～」。◆ work out 「籌畫,研擬」。亦有「計畫出,想出,作出」的意思。◆ any special arrangement 「任何特別的安排」。為了同行的人(your party)特別準備的情形,例如,替有身體障礙的兒童準備輪椅等。

7–12 對於希望參觀工廠的回函 129

讓學生在企業中短期的工作，從實際的工作中，提高教育的成果。此為職業學校請求對方公司接受學生實習的一封信。

Dear Sir,

Founded in 1904, Stackworth College is the oldest educational institution in the province, and is consistently ranked in Higher Learning magazine's authoritative Best Colleges list.

Two years ago, as part of our commitment to providing the best possible education for our students, we inaugurated a new Summer Internship Program in which students are able to earn credits for short-term work in local companies and enterprises.

The success of this Program has been overwhelming, and we have had more than three applicants for every place available.

I am writing to ask if your company would consider participating in this Program by accepting one (or preferably two) of our students for one three-month period each year. To fulfill the requirements of the course, the students must work at least four hours each day. In return for this work, students receive the token remuneration stipulated in the Program Guidelines, a copy of which I am enclosing with this letter.

Companies already participating in our Program include Shipman Engineering, Masters & Harris Associates, PriceRite Minimart, and Cornwell Design Studio.

All of these companies have expressed great satisfaction with the quality of the students we have sent them, and in some cases have offered students **full-time positions** after graduation.

I shall be delighted to send you any other information you might require about this Program.

Sincerely,

敬啟者：

　　創立於 1904 年的斯泰克渥滋學院，為本地最為古老的教育機構。並始終列名於由高等教育雜誌上所發表，極具權威性的「最佳高等學府」名單中。

　　為了對本校的學生盡可能地施以最完善的教育，同時也是我們的義務之一，我們於二年前，開始實施全新的「暑期教育實習課程」，讓學生藉由在本地的公司企業中短期的工作，以取得學分。

　　這項課程非常地成功，還有超過三位以上的申請者，申請一個空缺的情形。

　　在此徵詢貴公司，是否有意贊助此項課程計畫，每年以三個月為一期，接納我們的一名（可能的話二名）學生。為了符合這項教育實習課程的要求，學生每天至少需工作 4 個小時。至於工作的報酬方面，課程計畫中已載明學生們只領取象徵性質的薪資，隨函亦附上課程計畫的影本。

　　目前已加入我們實習課程的公司，包括史普門電機、哈利精英集團、普萊斯瑞特小型超市、康威爾設計工作室等。

　　以上的所有公司，皆對我們所送出的學生素質表示相當滿意。有些公司還提供了學生在畢業後的全職工作。

　　若您需要任何與此項課程計畫相關的資料，我們將很樂意為您寄上。

謹上

【語句注釋】◆ province 「地方」。在英國，倫敦以外的地方，全部稱為 province。加拿大的安大略省稱為 the Province of Ontario。◆ authoritative 「(資料等)可信賴的，具有權威的」。◆ commitment 「義務，責任」。◆ inaugurate 「開始，正式發起」。◆ program 「教育課程」。◆ fulfill the requirements of the course 「符合此課程的要求」。requirements 「必要條件，資格」。fulfill the requirements for graduation (符合畢業的各項條件)。◆ token 「象徵性的，形式上的」。◆ remuneration 「報酬」。◆ stipulate 「載明，規定」。◆ full-time position 「全職的職務」。a full-time job (全職(專任)的工作)。

自己也是該校的畢業生，在能做到的範圍內，自然很樂意接受實習生，但是因為公司實在太小，恐怕無法給予學生實地的教育與指導，以此為主旨的回信。

Dear Mr. Grimshaw,

It was with great interest that I read your letter about the new Stackworth College Summer Internship Program. I myself graduated from Stackworth in 1967, and I wish such a program had been available when I was a student.

I am not sure, however, that Prototype Publishing is the kind of company you are looking for. We have only six employees, four of whom work at home.

We would not be in a position to give the kind of on-site training and guidance emphasized in your Program Guidelines.

Yours sincerely,

格林修先生大鑒:

　　本人至感興趣地拜讀了您寄來的關於斯泰克渥滋學院的「暑期實習教育課程」的信函。我自己本身也於 1967 年畢業於斯泰克渥滋學院。真希望我還是學生時,就有此類課程。

　　然而,我不確定典範出版社是否為您所尋求的公司類型。目前我們只有六名員工,其中有四位在家中工作。

　　我們恐怕無法提供如課程計劃中所強調的實地的現場指導及訓練。

謹上

【語句注釋】◆ **I wish such a program had been available**　「真希望在過去也有諸如此類的課程」。I wish + 假定子句,在此乃對過去事情的假定。◆ **look for**　「期待,找尋」。◆ **on-site training**　「現場訓練」。on-site 也可用 on-the-spot 替代。on-site inspection(現場檢查)、on-the-spot report(現場的報告)、on-the-job training(實地的訓練實習)。

8

人 事

對於突然的調職感到非常吃驚。因為自己對於本地的職務非常滿意，詢問此異動是基於什麼考量下所決定的信。

Dear Mr. Williams:

I was deeply disturbed to learn that I am due to be transferred to the Boston Branch in April.

The announcement of the transfer came as a complete surprise. As you know, I have worked in the Washington Branch for over six years, and have been very happy here. I am not sure upon what basis the transfer decision was taken, or why I was not consulted in the matter.

I ask you to reconsider this decision. If my services are no longer required here in Washington, I am prepared to submit my resignation.

Yours truly,

威廉斯先生台鑒：

　　獲知本人將於 4 月被調職到波士頓分公司之事，著實令我非常地困擾。

　　此調職的通告來得十分地突然。如您所知，本人已於華盛頓分公司服務了 6 年以上的時間，並相當滿意目前的工作。我不知道此異動是基於什麼考量下決定的，或者，為何不曾與本人就此事討論過？

　　希望您能重新考慮此一決定。若華盛頓分公司已不再需要本人的服務，我將準備提出辭呈。

　　　　　　　　　　　　　　　　　　　　　　　　　　謹上

【語句注釋】◆ due 「預定（做）～的，預期的」。◆ I am happy here. 「我在此地很滿意。」◆ reconsider 「重新考慮」。◆ services 「工作，貢獻，盡力」。作此意解時，常使用複數形。「售後服務」為 after-sale services，而「那家公司所生產的產品『售後服務』很好」則必須說 The company provides good service on their products.◆ be prepared to ～ 「準備～，有～的心理準備」。◆ submit 「提出」。

【注意】以我們的習慣來說，通常要書寫此類信件相當地不容易。或許最多可質問到為何沒有事前通知等的程度。然而，若要詢問到底基於什麼標準，即使問了，公司方面也不會答覆。因為在不景氣時，公司有時會藉由人事的調動，迂迴地暗示某人自動請辭。但願今後隨著就業市場狀況的改變，也能與歐美同步，對自己的能力有信心的人，能夠積極地提出如此的質詢，放聲說道：「若不依我的要求，本人就辭職！」

　　因自己在同一辦事處已工作了 6 年之久，希望利用公司的新調職制度，申請轉調的信。

Dear Mr. Howe:

Although I have enjoyed working at the Toronto office of Barrington Securities for the last six years, I should like to take advantage of the company's new reassignment program and apply for a transfer to another office.

Although I understand that application for a transfer does not necessarily guarantee reassignment to the office of my choice, my personal preference would be for a posting to one of the two Barrington Securities offices in British Columbia.

Sincerely,

霍爾先生台鑒：

　　本人雖已在巴林頓證券的多倫多辦事處愉快地工作了 6 年之久，但我希望藉由公司新設立的調職制度，申請調往其他辦事處。

　　雖然本人了解到，申請調職並不一定可轉調到所希望的辦事處，但我個人希望能被分配到英屬哥倫比亞巴林頓證券的二家辦事處之一。

　　　　　　　　　　　　　　　　　　　　　　　　　　　謹上

【語句注釋】◆ securities 「證券」。◆ take advantage of 「利用」。另外，此片語也有「占便宜」的含意，使用時要注意。◆ reassignment program 「調職制度」。assignment 指「任務的分擔」，reassignment 則意為「重新分配工作」。◆ transfer 「調職，轉任」。◆ personal preference 「個人的意願」。◆ posting 「（職務的）任命」。

調任之際，對新工作地點和繼任者的介紹，並對於在任期間承蒙對方的善意協助與親切接待表示謝意的一封信。

Dear Mr. Timberley,

I am writing to let you know that I have been assigned to the post of Executive Manager of the Product Development Section of our Taiwan Office.

Although I am looking forward to the challenge of this new assignment, it will be difficult indeed to leave behind the friends and colleagues I have made here in Australia.

My place here in the Sydney Office will be taken by Mr. Robinson, formerly the Assistant Manager of our Perth Bureau, and I am sure you will be hearing from him very shortly.

I should like to thank you for all the kindnesses you extended to me during my three-year stay in Australia, and only wish I could have an opportunity to repay these kindnesses at some time in the future.

Please do not fail to contact me if you should ever find yourself in Taiwan.

Yours sincerely,

汀柏利先生台鑒：

　　謹在此向您報告，本人已被任命為臺灣辦事處產品開發部執行經理一職。

　　雖然我對此新職務相當地期待，但在另一方面，對於自己在澳洲所結識的朋友及同事，亦感到十分地不捨。

　　本人在雪梨辦事處所擔任的職務，將由前任伯斯分處的副理羅賓森先生接手。相信他將很快地與您聯繫。

　　在澳大利亞服務的 3 年中，很感謝您對我的照顧。只希望在將來有機會能回報此深情。

　　若您有機會來到臺灣，請務必與我聯絡。

謹上

【語句注釋】◆ be assigned to the post of 「被任命～之職」。◆ the challenge of this new assignment 「新任命的工作」。challenge 在此與其說是「挑戰」，倒不如解作「值得奮鬥的工作，努力的目標」之意更為妥切。◆ leave behind 「將～留下，置之而去」。leave ～ behind 的句型也常使用。You can leave your heavy suitcase behind.（你可以留下那隻沈重的手提箱）。◆ My place will be taken by 「我的職務將由～繼任」。take ～'s place「承繼（該作的）工作、職務、任務等」。其他類似的用法有 take place「發生」、take the place of ～「取代～」等。◆ to repay these kindness 「回報如此厚意」。repay 亦可用 reciprocate 替代。◆ Please do not fail to contact me 「請務必與我聯絡」。◆ if you should ever find yourself in Taiwan 「若您有機會來到臺灣」。

對於對方即將調職離去一事表示遺憾，除了感謝一路共事而來，同時恭賀對方擢昇新職。更進一步表示，若有機會拜訪，一定會和對方聯絡等內容的信。

Dear Mr. Wu,

I was sorry to hear that you will be leaving Sydney and returning to Japan.

I am sure that I **speak for everyone here** at Simmons & Bentley when I say that we shall be extremely sad to see you go. It was always a pleasure doing business with you, and **your warm personality** and lively sense of humour **were very much appreciated**.

Although you do not say as much in your letter, I know that your transfer to Taiwan is a significant promotion for you, and a major step forward in your career. Please accept my heartiest congratulations.

I don't have any plans for visiting Taiwan **in the foreseeable future**, but **rest assured that if my path ever takes me to Taiwan**, I shall certainly give you a call.

Yours sincerely,

吳先生大鑒:

　　很遺憾聽到您將離開雪梨，返回臺灣的消息。

　　深信本人可代表西蒙班利公司全體同仁表示，得知您將返國的消息，對我們將是一件極為難過的事。與您共事總是那麼的和樂，大家對於您善體人意的個人特質及活潑的幽默感都非常地欣賞。

　　雖然您在來信中並未著墨太多，但我相信此次調任臺灣，對您而言，必是十分重要的擢昇，並在您的職業生涯中邁進了一大步。在此獻上我最衷心的恭賀。

　　目前本人並沒有任何造訪臺灣的計畫。將來若有機會到臺灣，必定打電話通知您。

　　　　　　　　　　　　　　　　　　　　　　　　　謹上

【語句注釋】◆ I speak for everyone here 「謹代表公司全體同仁表示」。for 有「代表，代替」之意。◆ your warm personality 「您善體人意的人格特質」。◆ be very much appreciated 「備受欣賞」。appreciate 亦有「感謝」之意，故在商業書信中，We would appreciate it if you would ～「若您能～則甚幸」，為常用句型。◆ in the foreseeable future 「目前（沒有～的打算），在可預測的未來」之意，此片語多與否定句一起使用。◆ rest assured that ～ 「必定會～」。◆ if my path ever takes me to Taiwan 「若到臺灣時」。字面上的直譯則為「～道路將我帶到某地點」之意。

【注意】若某人的調職很明顯的為昇職時，千萬別忘了表示祝賀之意。

8-5 向公司提出離職的通知

雖已討論過種種問題，自己仍決定在 1 個月後離開公司，並請公司在此期間尋找繼任人選的信。

Dear Mr. Norwood:

It was very kind of you to take the time to see me yesterday afternoon, and discuss with me the problems I have been having in the Planning Section.

Although I appreciate your consideration in offering me a transfer to the Accounts Office, I still feel that it would be better for everyone concerned if I left Plastronics Incorporated and found a position with another company.

I understand that my sudden departure might inconvenience the staff of the Planning Section, and I am prepared to continue working another month to give you time to find a replacement.

Yours faithfully,

8-6 辭呈

請辭時向公司提出的書信。

Dear Mr. Thomas:

I wish to resign my present position with Bell Corporation, the resignation effective as of July 31.

Yours faithfully,

諾伍德先生大鑒：

　　很感謝您昨日下午特地抽出時間與我討論，本人在企畫部中所面臨的種種問題。

　　感謝您建議我可以調職到會計部門。但本人仍覺得還是離開普利斯東尼克公司，到其他公司另覓新職，對所有相關的人都好。

　　我了解自己若突然離職，將對企畫部的同仁造成不便，故我準備繼續工作1個月，給您些許時間尋找繼任人選。

　　　　　　　　　　　　　　　　　　　　　　　　　　　　謹上

【語句注釋】◆ It is kind of you to ～ 「很感謝您好意～」。◆ Planning Section 「企畫部」。◆ inconvenience 「給～帶來困擾，使～感到不便」。在此 inconvenience 為動詞。

湯瑪斯先生大鑒：

　　茲在此請辭本人目前於貝爾公司之職務，並於 7 月 31 日起生效。

　　　　　　　　　　　　　　　　　　　　　　　　　　　　謹上

最近公司的業績惡化，經由為了裁減人員所設計的提早退休制度，自己已於 3 月份離開公司，然因 53 歲的自己仍能工作，希望可以繼續就業，貢獻自己的經驗為主要內容的信。

Dear Mr. Tomlinson,

It has been some time since I last wrote to you. A lot has been happening, and I have been extremely busy.

As I may have mentioned when we met in Baton Rouge last year, Orchard Electronics has been going through a rather difficult patch recently. We failed to secure two very important Middle East contracts in August, and one of our biggest Korean suppliers went bankrupt in October.

In order to survive in what is becoming an increasingly more competitive market, Orchard has had to cut back on new personnel appointments, and has offered senior staff the option of early retirement with full benefits. Though it was a very difficult decision to make, after much consideration, and long discussion with my wife Mary, I decided to take up the early retirement option.

On March 31 I left Orchard, and for the last month I have been enjoying my new-found leisure and thinking about the future. Fifty-three is, I feel, a little too early to call it a day. If possible, I would like to find a similar position in another company, and put my marketing experience to use for another few years.

Although I no longer work for Orchard, I sincerely hope that we will be able to keep in touch and, **who knows**, perhaps we will have an opportunity to meet again either in the States or here in Taiwan.

Yours sincerely,

湯姆林森先生台鑒：

　　距離上回寫信與您，已過了一段時間。在這段期間，我經歷了許多事情，也一直相當忙碌。

　　正如去年我們在巴頓魯治會面時，本人或許已提過的，歐查德電子公司最近正面臨相當困難的處境。在 8 月時，我們沒有成功地確保在中東的二份非常重要的契約。更甚，我們最大的一家韓國零件供應廠商，也於 10 月份宣告破產。

　　為了在競爭日益激烈的市場上生存，歐查德不得已削減新進人員的錄用，並以全額的補助鼓勵資深人員提早退休。

　　雖然難以決定，但在自己深思熟慮，以及與內人瑪麗的反覆商談後，我選擇了提早退休。

　　我已於 3 月 31 日離開歐查德。過去這 1 個月來，我在享受全新的閒暇，同時，也一直考慮著將來。對我而言，以 53 歲之齡結束事業生涯，未免尚嫌太早。可能的話，希望能在其他公司找到類似的職務，應用自己的市場經驗，再發揮幾年。

　　雖然我已不再為歐查德工作，仍很希望我們繼續保持聯絡，說不定，我們將來或許有機會在美國或臺灣此地再相見呢。

謹上

【語句注釋】◆ **some time** 「相當長的一段時間」。用作此意時，重音在 some，若重音放在 time 的話，則指「短暫的時間」之意。例如：They talked for some time.（他們談了相當長的一段時間）、It may be some time before we meet again.（或許我們不久就會再相見。）◆ **a lot** 「許多（人、事物。）a lot of ～，lots of ～ 的句型，也常使用。◆ **go through a difficult patch** 「面臨難關」。go through「經歷困難」。patch 指「時期，期間」，通常伴隨著 bad、difficult、sticky 等形容詞，表示「艱困的時期」。◆ **suppliers** 「零件製造商」。◆ **cut back on ～** 「削減～」。◆ **new personnel appointment** 「新進人員的錄用」。◆ **early retirement** 「提早退休」。◆ **benefits** 「給付金，津貼」。retirement benefits「退休金」。◆ **new-found** 「新發現到的」。◆ **call it a day** 「結束（當天的工作），收工」。Let's call it a night!（今天晚上到此為止！）◆ **put ～ to use** 「利用～」。◆ **who knows** 「誰知道，說不定」。

8-8　離職通知的回函

　　收到朋友般的工作往來對象的離職通知信後，致上鼓勵話語的書信。

Dear Mr. Bailey,

Your letter of May 7 came as a tremendous surprise. I had no idea that things were so bad at Orchard Electronics. Last month we had a visit from Tom Pickins, the local representative of your main distributor here in the South, and he didn't mention anything about the kind of difficulties you describe in your letter. As far as I can see, Orchard products are still selling well in our market, though some of the newer OEM brands are, it's true, attracting a lot of consumer attention.

I can fully sympathize with your mixed feelings about early retirement. I would have thought that lots of other companies would be only too eager to snap up someone like yourself, with three decades of hands-on experience in overseas marketing.

If I hear of any jobs going, I shall of course let you know, but I'm afraid my contacts are all local, and my background is in retail sales.

Please rest assured that I am just as eager as you are to maintain our long and close friendship. I am sure we will meet again, God willing, and not before very long.

Yours sincerely,

貝利先生台鑒:

　　收到您於 5 月 7 日的來信，大吃了一驚。我一點也不知道貴公司歐查德電子的情況這麼糟糕。上個月，貴公司南方總經銷商的駐地代表湯姆‧匹金斯到本公司訪問時，並沒有提到任何如您信中描述的困難。就我目前所觀察，歐查德的產品在我們的市場仍銷售得很好。不過確實有許多原廠委託加工製造的新品牌產品也相當受到顧客的青睞。

　　本人對您提早退休的複雜心情，完全能夠理解。不過，像在海外市場具有 30 年實務經驗的您，想必有許多其他公司對您求才若渴。

　　我若有任何職缺的消息，一定會告訴您。不過恐怕我所接觸的範圍，僅限於本地。而且，我的工作背景也僅限於零售業。

　　我也和您同樣渴望繼續保持我們長久以來的深厚友誼。並深信若有機會的話，我們在不久之後會再相見。

謹上

【語句注釋】◆ **had no idea** 「完全不知道」。didn't know at all 意思也大致相同。◆ **so bad** 「(如您所說的)這麼糟糕」。◆ **local representative** 「駐地代表」。representative 常用於業務人員。◆ **are still selling well** 「現在仍銷售得很好」。在此 sell 為「銷售」之意的不及物動詞。are still (being) sold well 的情況,則有在人為的努力下被推銷的感覺,若欲表現因產品本身優良而(自然地)銷售出的語感時,一定要使用不及物動詞。◆ **OEM brand** 「原廠委託加工製造的品牌」。OEM 為 original equipment manufacturing 的縮寫,為製造商不採用自己的商標,而以下訂單的原廠的商標掛名製造的委託生產方式。◆ **sympathize with ～** 「對～有同感」。sympathize 經常譯為「同情」,但在此解作「了解～的心情」,應較貼切。◆ **I would have thought that lots of other companies would be only too eager to ～** 「其他的許多公司,想必正引頸期盼以待(挖角)～」。I think that …will be too eager to ～的說法在意思上亦大致相同,不過在此因含有 I am not sure 的語氣,故以假設法表現。◆ **snap up** 「搶先錄用,擢用」。◆ **hands-on experience** 「實務的經驗」。指非紙上談兵,而為實際上的經驗。◆ **If I hear of any jobs going ～** 「若聽到徵才的消息的話～」。在此,go 為「開始動作,產生需求」之意,此處的 going 大致與 available 同義。any jobs 為 of 的受詞,going 為受詞補語。◆ **I shall ～** 「我將～」。美式用法,shall 表堅決、強硬的意志。◆ **close friendship** 「親密的友情」。在此 close 為適當的用詞,絕對不用 intimate。◆ **God willing** 「上天若允許,有機會的話」。分詞片語,意同 if God is willing。

【注意】在此信中雖以 God willing 表現,不過因有關於宗教,使用時最好要注意。例如若知道對方為虔誠的天主教徒,而自己卻是無神論者的情形時,此表現聽來就有點虛假。這和不對佛教國家寄出寫著 Merry Christmas 的卡片,是一樣的道理。

先前的書信中（範例 8-7），告訴了友人，自己提前退休，正在找尋新工作的狀況。此次則是通知友人自己已經找到了新工作，並期待今後有機會赴美洽公時能再相見的一封信。

Dear Mr. Tomlinson,

Many thanks for your kind and **comforting** letter of May 15. One of the reasons it has taken me so long to **respond** is that I have been extremely **busy looking for** a job here in Taipei.

I am happy to say that I am now in the final stages of negotiations with a small manufacturer of electric motors, and if all goes well, I shall **take up a position** in their export department from June 1.

Shortly after writing to you in May, I received an offer of a job with a large trading company. Although the pay and conditions were far better than I could have expected, considering my age and my background, I decided to decline the offer and **go for** the position with the electric motor manufacturer. Perhaps the biggest reason was job content. The work I would have had to do at the trading company would have been almost all clerical, and I would have had to work alongside people half my age. At the motor manufacturer, however, I shall be completely **in charge of** the new export department, and **responsible** only to the managing director.

Ta-ming Electric Motors (the name of the company I shall be joining) has been supplying small electric motors to Taiwanese precision instrument firms for many years now, and Mr. Wang, the **managing director**, would like to open up new markets abroad. He has asked me to set up a small export department, and has appointed two young staff members to work under me.

I am still unable to believe my luck in finding a job so soon, and one that will give me a chance to make full use of my business experience and personal contacts. Our first target will be the European market, but all being well, we will begin to research the American market sometime next year, and I may have occasion to visit the States at that time. Perhaps we shall be able to meet again much sooner than expected!

Yours sincerely,

湯姆林森先生台鑒:

　　非常感謝您在 5 月 15 日寄來的親切及鼓勵的來信。我之所以拖了這麼久而尚未回信的原因之一，乃是為了在臺北謀職，因而極為忙碌。

　　幸運地，我和一家小型的電動馬達製造商之間的面談，已進入最後階段。若一切順利的話，我將由 6 月 1 日起，在此公司的外銷部門工作。

　　在 5 月寫信給您之後不久，有一家大型的貿易公司，願意給我一份工作。雖然所提供的薪資及其他條件，都遠比我期待的還好得許多，然而在考慮到自己的年齡和經歷後，我婉拒了他們的邀請，決定選擇電動馬達製造商。或許最大的理由，是在於工作的成就感。若在貿易公司工作，則幾乎所有的工作都是文書性質，而且同事的年齡只有我的一半。然而，在馬達製造商的公司中，我將完全負責新成立的外銷部門，上司只有總經理一人。

　　大明電動馬達（我即將前往就職的公司名），多年來一直供應臺灣國內的精密儀器公司小型的電動馬達。現在，總經理王先生希望能拓

展新的海外市場。他希望我能設立一小型的外銷部門，並且還安排了二名年輕僱員，在我旗下工作。

　　至今仍無法相信，自己能在這麼短的時間內，幸運地找到一個能完全地活用自己的實務經驗以及人脈的工作。我們首要的目標雖為歐洲的市場，但若一切進行順利的話，將在明年開始進行美國市場的調查。屆時，可能將有赴美的機會。我們或許會比預期還要早碰面呢！

謹上

【語句注釋】◆ comforting 「鼓勵的，安慰的」。◆ respond 「回信，回應」。也可用 reply。◆ busy looking for 「忙於尋找～」。busy in looking for ～的意思。在此 in 指「在～時候，當～之際」的意思。不過通常將 in 省略，成為 busy ～ing 的句型。◆ take up a position 「就任」。◆ go for ～ 「去追求～」。◆ in charge of ～ 「擔任～，負責～」。用於對某事負有責任的人。◆ responsible to ～ 「對～負責，在～的掌控下」。◆ managing director 「總經理，公司負責人」。在英國有時使用 president 一詞。◆ open up a new market 「開拓新市場」。◆ set up 「設立，開設」。大體上與 establish 相同。

通知對方已獲准入會 Friday Club，若有意入會，請逕辦理入會手續的一封信。

Dear Mr. Yoshida:

I am pleased to inform you that Messrs. Albert Connington and Allen Watson have submitted your name to the Friday Club **membership committee**, and have agreed to act as sponsors.

As you may know, the Friday Club is one of the oldest and most **exclusive** associations in the Frampton area. Membership is by invitation only, and invitations are extended only to citizens of Frampton who have made **outstanding** contributions to the business and commercial life of the city. In their **submission** to the membership committee, Messrs. Connington and Watson emphasized your **key role** in bringing new business and new jobs to the area, and your many contributions to **local charities**.

The membership committee, **of which I am chairperson**, has unanimously approved the submission, and has directed me to extend an official invitation to you.

If you would care to accept the invitation to join the Friday Club, would you please complete the enclosed forms and return them to me at your convenience.

Yours faithfully,

吉田先生大鑒：

　　很高興地在此告知，亞爾勃特・康寧頓先生以及艾倫・華生先生已向 Friday Club 會員遴選委員會呈交您的大名，並同意作為您的入會保證人。

　　如您所知，Friday Club 是佛蘭普敦地區最古老且最高級的協會之一。惟有經由本協會的邀請方可入會。而且邀請入會的對象僅限於在本市經貿活動中有顯著貢獻的佛蘭普敦市民。在康寧頓和華生二位先生向會員遴選委員會提交的推薦書中，他們強調了您在為地方帶來新商機及新的就業機會方面，扮演了重要的角色，此外，還對本地的慈善事業，有許多的貢獻。

　　由本人擔任主席的會員遴選委員會，全體一致同意您的入會申請，並由我向您致上正式的邀請函。

　　若您願意接受加入 Friday Club 的邀請，請填好隨函附上的表格。並在您方便時，將申請表回寄給本人。

謹上

【語句注釋】◆ **membership committee** 「會員遴選委員會，人事委員會」。◆ **exclusive** 「嚴格選擇會員的；上流社會的」之意的形容詞。exclusive 原來就有排除不合標準者的意思，因此會使用在諸如此類的詞語中。在商業上，經常使用exclusive distributor（獨家經銷店；特約店）。◆ **outstanding** 「顯著的」。另外也有「未付清的」之意。◆ **submission** 「提議，提案」。◆ **key role** 「重要角色」。也可說成 important part。英文也有 a key person（關鍵人物）等的說法。◆ **local charity** 「地方上的慈善活動」。◆ **of which I am chairperson** 「（會員遴選委員會的）主席」。若只將此部分取出，寫成完整句子，則成為 "I am chairperson of the membership committee." 雖也可用 the chair(person)，但指特定組織的首長而且只有一位時，通常不加冠詞。

對於 Friday Club 的入會邀請，表示接受的信。

Dear Mr. Cassidy,

I have heard about the Frampton Friday Club from many friends and business associates, and the invitation to join the Club came as a singular honor.

I shall be delighted to accept the invitation, and I am returning the forms you asked me to fill in.

In the section on other affiliations, I have written a couple of Japanese names. The Seiryu-no-kai is a small association of businessmen in the Kansai area, and the Kokusaiboeki-kenkyukai is a study group I formed when I was a graduate student at Miki University, and of which I am still the honorary chairman.

Sincerely,

卡西迪先生大鑒：

　　從許多朋友及同業口中，久聞佛蘭普敦 Friday Club 之大名。能受到您的邀請入會，本人感到無比的光榮。

　　我很樂意地接受這項邀請，並寄回您希望我填好的表格。

　　在「其他所屬團體」一欄中，我寫了二個日本的會名。「清流協會」為關西地區的小型商業界人士的集會，另外，「國際貿易研究會」則是本人還是三木大學的研究所學生時組成的一個研究會，現在我仍為此研究會的名譽會長。

謹上

【語句注釋】◆ **business associate** 「生意上的夥伴」。◆ **singular** 「非凡的，無比的」。◆ **fill in** 「填寫（表格）」。也可說 fill out。◆ **on other affiliations** 「有關其他所屬團體」。在此情況，on 和 about 同義。◆ **a graduate (student)** 「研究所學生」。大學學生為 an undergraduate (student)。◆ **honorary chairman** 「名譽會長」。

8-12 人才的挖角

對曾於共同的開發計畫中合作過的對象，提出邀請的書信。

Dear Tom:

Now that the first stage of the D.Y.P. Project is behind us, I want to let you know what a pleasure it was working with you in Osaka, Atlanta, and on site in the Philippines.

Over the years, I have worked on similar development projects with teams from many different companies, and I cannot recall a project that has gone as smoothly, and has been as trouble-free, as this one.

Without a doubt, the biggest reason for the success was the skill you demonstrated in handling the numerous problems that came up. I think the Feya Corporation is indeed fortunate to have secured the services of such a talented and resourceful manager as yourself.

Speaking frankly, Davidson & Morley is always on the lookout for managers of your caliber, and should you ever consider a mid-career change, I would be delighted to discuss the matter with you in the strictest confidence.

Please give my best regards to Tony, Kenny, Scott, and all the other members of your exceptional team.

Sincerely,

親愛的湯姆：

因為 D.Y.P. 開發計畫的第一階段已告尾聲，在此希望讓您知道，能與您在大阪、亞特蘭大及目前在菲律賓一起工作，是多麼愉快的一件事。

多年來，我曾經和來自許多不同公司的隊伍合作過很多類似的開發計畫。而在我的記憶中，沒有一次像這次一樣進行得如此順利，如此地近乎「零缺點」。

無庸置疑的，此回成功的最大因素，在於您對產生的諸多問題的處理上，所展現的能力。能擁有如閣下如此既有才能且富機智的經理人才，飛雅公司真是幸運。

坦白說，戴維森摩利公司，一直在尋覓像您如此具有才華的人。因此，若您有轉職的念頭，本人將很樂意在極其保密的情形下，與您討論該事宜。

請代為向東尼、肯尼、史考特以及貴公司優秀的工作小組的其他成員，致問候之意。

謹上

【語句注釋】◆ Now that ～ 「因為～」。與 since 的意思大致上相同。◆ what a pleasure it was working with you 「與您一起工作相當的愉快」。在此 what 為感嘆詞，與 how much（多麼的、非常的）相同。it 為形式主詞，指 working with you。◆ on site 「當地（發生）的」。◆ over the years 「多年來」。也有「隨著時間的過去」之意。◆ recall 「想起，回憶起」。語義和 remember 大致相同。◆ this one 「這一次，此回」。指 this project。◆ demonstrate 「展現，顯示」。此處的語義與 show 大致相同。◆ resourceful 「富於機智的，策略高明的」。◆ caliber 「才識」。英式拼法為 calibre。◆ mid-career change 「轉職」。◆ in the strictest confidence 「極度保密的」。◆ exceptional 「非常優秀的，超凡的」。

感謝在共同開發計畫中予以自己如此高的評價，並表示對於跳槽的邀請，希望給與一段時間考慮的信。

Dear Kevin:

Many thanks for your letter, and the kind things you had to say about my participation in the D.Y.P. Project.

I believe the success of any such project depends on teamwork, and teamwork depends on mutual trust and understanding. I found it very easy to communicate with you and your staff, and being able to speak openly about every aspect of the project helped to avoid much of the misunderstanding that often plagues joint ventures between companies.

I feel honored that you should rate my work so highly, and that you would be prepared to discuss a mid-career change with me. I have been with Feya for over fifteen years now. Although my career with them has had its ups and downs. I cannot say that I am dissatisfied with my present position, either from the point of view of job content or salary. On the other hand, I do find the prospect of a new challenge a very attractive one.

This is a matter I need time to think about, and I would also like to talk it over with my wife the next time I am back in Taiwan. That will probably be at the end of this month, and I will certainly write to you again at the beginning of April.

Best regards,

親愛的凱文:

　　感謝您的來信，以及信中對本人參與 D.Y.P. 開發計畫的嘉許。

　　我相信任何計畫的成功均仰賴於團隊合作，而團隊合作則有賴於相互的信賴與瞭解。我發現與您和您的人員溝通非常容易，而且能夠就此計畫各方面開誠佈公的討論，有助於避免企業合作中，常造成困擾的許多誤解。

　　對您給與我的工作如此高的評價，還準備和本人討論跳槽一事，感到十分榮幸。到目前為止，我已於飛雅工作 15 年以上。其中雖也有起有落，但就現職來說，無論是工作的成就感或薪資而言，也不能說不滿意。但另一方面，您所提及的新工作前景，還是十分地吸引我。

　　對跳槽一事，我需要一些時間考慮，並且希望在下一次回臺灣時，與內人討論。那應該會在本月底左右，故我會在 4 月初時再與您聯絡。

　　　　　　　　　　　　　　　　　　　　　　　　　　　　謹上

【語句注釋】◆ the kind things you had to say 「您客氣親切的話語」。與 the kind things you said 的說法在內容上雖相同，但如此迂迴的表現時，可表示謙虛，並含有感謝的心情。◆ plague 「使煩擾」。在此為動詞。◆ you should rate ～ 「給與～的評價」。should 一詞，表示「驚訝，意料之外」，也可說有表示謙虛的含意。◆ discuss a mid-career change with me 「和我討論轉職跳槽一事」。discuss 為及物動詞，注意後面直接接受詞，而不用 discuss about ～。◆ I have been with Feya 「我已在飛雅公司服務了～(年)」。在此 with 表示「服務」。◆ ups and downs 「變動，浮沈」。◆ find the prospect of a new challenge a very attractive one 「認為新工作的前景非常有吸引力」。在此 find 為不完全及物動詞，the prospect of a new challenge 為受詞，a very attractive one (= challenge) 則為受詞補語。◆ talk it over 「討論某事」。◆ That will probably be ～ 「那大概在～」。在此 that 指「與妻子商量」一事。

9

徵信查詢

　　最近市場上有家公司，四處調查有關貴公司的情況。至於他們的來歷背景、目的等，目前並不清楚。希望能及早通知貴公司以便有所防範的一封信。

Dear Mr. Matsumoto,

I hope that your trip to Thailand was an enjoyable one, and that you were able to secure a contract with a local supplier.

I am writing to you this time with regard to a rather sensitive matter, and I trust that you will keep it in the strictest confidence.

It has been brought to my attention that someone has been making inquiries about your company here in Vancouver. Last week my office received a letter asking about our business relations with you, moreover, two of my staff members have told me that the same subject was brought up during informal luncheons with employees of other firms.

At the moment I have no clear idea who is making these inquiries, or indeed why they are doing so. I thought it better, however, to let you know about them as soon as possible. If I do get hold of any other information in this matter, I shall of course contact you immediately.

Yours sincerely,

松本先生台鑒：

　　希望您的泰國之行相當盡興，並且成功地與當地的供應商簽約。

　　我這次之所以寫信給您，乃是關於一件相當敏感的事情，我相信您會將此事列為最高機密。

　　我注意到最近有人在溫哥華打聽貴公司的情況，我的辦公室上個禮拜收到了一封詢問我們雙方在生意上的關係的信。還有，我的二位同事告訴我，在與其他公司員工的非正式午餐聚會上，也提到了相同的話題。

　　目前，我完全不清楚到底是誰在進行這些調查，或者到底有什麼目的，但我卻覺得應該儘可能地及早讓您知道才是。若我得知其他有關此事的任何訊息，一定會立刻通知您。

　　　　　　　　　　　　　　　　　　　　　　　　謹上

【語句注釋】◆ secure a contract 「獲得契約」。◆ a local supplier 「當地的供應商（製造商等）」。◆ a rather sensitive matter 「相當敏感的話題（事情）」。sensitive 指「微妙的，須注意的」。◆ keep it in the strictest confidence 「列為最高的機密」。◆ it has been brought to my attention that ～ 「我注意到（察覺到）～」。◆ make inquiries about ～ 「詢問有關～」。◆ the same subject was brought up 「提到相同的話題」。the same subject 指某人對貴公司的詢問與調查。◆ I have no clear idea 「我完全不知道」。◆ get hold of 「手中握有～」。hold 為名詞，指「掌握，握持」。◆ in this matter 「有關此事件」。in ～「有關～，針對～，就～而言」。

對於能迅速獲知公司正受到其他公司的不明調查一事表示感謝，也更加確立了彼此之間的信賴關係。回函除了答謝對方的來函通知，也一併表示將密切注意此不明調查的後續動向。

Dear Mr. Manzi,

I am deeply obliged to you for informing me about the inquiries someone is making about Top Merit in Vancouver.

I feel honored that you should have chosen to share such sensitive information with me, and am confident that your considerate gesture has created an even stronger bond between our two companies.

I have a fairly good idea who is behind the inquiries. One of our major competitors here in Osaka is attempting to expand into the North American market, and it could be that they are investigating existing distributorships in your area. It could also be that they are thinking of setting up their own arrangements with reliable, old-established distributors such as yourself.

If you should receive a direct approach from them, I would appreciate it if you could let me know as soon as possible.

Yours truly,

曼茲先生台鑒：

　　在此對您來信通知我關於有人正於溫哥華打聽 Top Merit 一事，深表感謝。

　　您決定與我分享這樣的機密情報，使我深感榮幸，我也確信您如此替人著想、考慮周詳的通知，已為我們雙方奠定了更穩固的關係。

　　此調查的幕後主使是誰，我們已相當清楚。我們在大阪本地的一家主要競爭公司，正準備拓展北美的市場。因此，或許是該公司想調查貴地區目前現有的經銷商競爭的狀況，也或許他們正考慮更進一步地與像貴公司一樣值得信賴、歷史悠久的經銷商簽署合作協定。

　　如果該公司直接與貴公司接觸，若能承蒙您儘速地通知我方，至感是幸。

　　　　　　　　　　　　　　　　　　　　　　　　　　　　謹上

【語句注釋】◆ be deeply obliged to ～　「對～深深感謝」。◆ feel honored that～「對～感到榮幸」。◆ share such sensitive information with　「與～共享如此機密的情報」。sensitive「有關機密的」。◆ considerate gesture　「思慮周詳的態度、表示」。gesture「姿態，示意」。◆ expand into　「向～擴展、往～拓展」。◆ it could be that「或許，可能是～」。◆ set up their own arrangement with～　「與～訂立他們自己的協定」。arrangement「協定，協商，決定」。make special arrangement with「與～訂定特別約定」。◆ old-established distributors　「老字號的經銷商」。

【注意】雖然公司與公司之間只是公事上的合作夥伴，但若彼此有著如家族般的密切良好關係，則可相互強化彼此的信賴。若市場上有任何風吹草動則可馬上互相聯絡，藉此也可使合作的基礎更加穩固，不可動搖。

　　從應徵者寄來的履歷中，得知該人過去曾在某公司任職。此封信函除了煩請該公司告知此人服務期間及離職時的狀況之外，同時也保證會將此份資料作機密處理。

Dear Mr. Miller,

Thornville Associates has received a job application from Ms. Yoko Tanigawa of Nishi-Murayama 2–3–65, Karasawa City.

In her resume she states that she worked for your company from March 1995 to October 1996.

I should be grateful for any information you could give me about Ms. Tanigawa's time with your company, and the circumstances of her departure.

Please rest assured that any information you can give me will be treated in the strictest confidence.

Yours faithfully,

米勒先生大鑒:

　　本公司松威爾合作企業，收到了住在唐澤市西村山 2-3-65 的谷川洋子小姐的應徵信函。

　　她在履歷中表示，曾於 1995 年 3 月到 1996 年 10 月這段期間，在貴公司服務過。

　　不知可否麻煩您，提供谷川小姐在貴公司的服務情形及離職狀況的資料，本人將衷心感謝。

　　本人在此保證，您所提供的任何相關資料，將視為最高機密處理。敬請放心。

　　　　　　　　　　　　　　　　　　　　　　　　　　　謹上

【語句注釋】◆ a job application 「工作應徵信函，求職信函」。◆ resume 「履歷表」。◆ time with your company 「在貴公司服務的情形」。time 表示「當時的情形」。◆ circumstances of her departure 「離職時的情況，狀況」。departure「離去，撤退」。在此意義同 resignation「辭職」的意思。◆ Please rest assured that ～ 「保證～，敬請放心」。

9-3　調查履歷信函(1)　169

收到了查詢離職員工背景的來信，雖然該員工的工作態度和人際關係都有問題，離職狀況也屬負面，但基於人事保密的原則，無法向請求查詢的公司說明詳情的回函。

Dear Mr. Roberts,

I am in receipt of your inquiry about Ms. Yoko Tanigawa.

I have consulted with her immediate superior, and she informs me that Ms. Tanigawa's departure was not an amicable one. Please understand that I am not in a position to provide you with details, but I can say that her commitment to her work left much to be desired, and her relations with her co-workers were not of the best.

You ask about the circumstances of her departure. Again, it is not company policy to disclose details of personnel matters, but in consideration of the fact that you are considering employing Ms. Tanigawa, I feel obliged to tell you that she was asked to tender her resignation.

Yours faithfully,

羅伯茲先生大鑒：

　　本人已收到您對谷川洋子小姐的查詢信函。

　　我已和谷川小姐過去的直屬上司談過，她告訴我，谷川小姐的離職情況並不很圓滿。在此請您諒解，以本人的立場，無法提供您相關的細節，但我可以向您透露一點的是，她的工作態度，實須多加強，此外，她與同事之間的人際關係也不甚理想。

　　您詢問到有關她離職時的情況。再次向您表明，本公司向來不對外界公開關於人事資料的詳情。不過，為了顧及貴公司或許正準備採用谷川小姐的事實，我想我應該告訴您，她是在本公司的要求下提出辭呈的。

　　　　　　　　　　　　　　　　　　　　　　　　　謹上

【語句注釋】◆ in receipt of　「已收到～」。此說法雖在現代給人一種老舊的感覺，但在歐洲仍為人所使用。We are in receipt of your letter dated May 5th.「我們已收到您 5 月 5 日的來信」。◆ immediate superior　「直屬上司」。◆ an amicable one　「圓滿（的狀況）」。amicable 含「友好的，和平的」之意。◆ her commitment to her work　「她的工作態度」。　commitment to～　「對～的投注、參與、獻身」。◆ left much to be desired「有許多遺憾之點，留有許多不滿意，尚有許多須加強之處」。much 為名詞，作 leave 的受詞。不定詞 to be desired 為形容詞性的用法，用來修飾 much。◆ in consideration of ～「在顧及～之下」。◆ consider　「考慮，深思」。注意不用 consider to employ。◆ feel obliged to ～　「認為應該～」。◆ tender her resignation　「提出辭呈」。

【注意】當內容關係到人事，寫信時必須非常小心。特別是對被查詢者的行為態度不滿意時，若回答得太詳細可能會對當事人造成負面的影響。對正準備僱用當事人的公司完全吐露詳情，對方也會心存恐懼。不過重要的事項，還是不能省略。

　　寄來履歷的應徵者在徵信對象欄裏填寫的是大學的教授。故去函請該教授就當事人的優缺點及是否適任應徵的職務等作簡略說明。

Dear Mr. Wilkins,

Mr. Junji Nakabayashi of 230 Green Heights, Nakano 3–1–1, Koto Ward, Tokyo has submitted your name as a reference for his application for the position of Assistant Systems Engineer in our company.

As Personnel Director of Cyber-Union Systems, could I please ask you to give me a brief summary of what you feel to be his strong and weak points, and if you think that he is suitable for the position for which he has applied.

Yours faithfully,

威爾金斯先生雅鑒:

　　住在東京都江東區中野 3–1–1 長春大樓 230 的中林順司先生,於日前應徵本公司之助理工程師一職,並在所提出的申請表中保證人一欄填寫了您的大名。

　　在此以塞柏聯合系統之人事主管的身分,不知是否可以請您就中林先生之優缺點,以及他是否能勝任所應徵的職務,作一簡短的結論說明。

　　　　　　　　　　　　　　　　　　　　　　　　　　　　謹上

當被詢問及自己教過的學生，由於該生在校時成績優秀，且自己對該生的性格也相當了解，故很樂意提筆回信。就連缺點的說明，依據角度的不同，也可視為優點。

Dear Mr. Hasegawa,

I am pleased to write in support of Mr. Junji Nakabayashi's application for a position at your company.

I have known Junji for over four years. He took my Advanced Programming I course in his second year at the Sanwa Technical College, and after graduation he often participated in my Applied Programming Seminar as an auditor.

If I had to summarize his strong points, I would say that he is highly motivated to succeed, and has the necessary concentration and stamina to attain any goal he sets himself. His grades at college were above average, and I have heard that he is very well thought of in his present workplace.

Like anyone, he also has a number of what might be called weak points. He needs to learn a little more patience in dealing with setbacks encountered in his work, and needs to temper his rather overwhelming sense of humor.

I must say, however, that such weak points are far outweighed by what I consider his many strong points, and I have no hesitation whatever in recommending him to you for the job he is seeking.
If you have any other questions about Junji, I shall be happy to answer them.

Yours faithfully,

長谷川先生台鑒：

　　很榮幸地以此信支持中林順司先生向貴公司所應徵之職務。

　　本人認識順司超過 4 年以上。他在三和工業大學二年級時，選修了我的一堂「高等程式設計」。畢業後，仍經常以旁聽生身分，出席我的「應用程式設計講習」課程。

　　若要簡短地陳述他的優點的話，他可說是凡事都相當熱誠，為了達成他自我設定的目標，具備了相當的集中力與耐力。他大學時的成績在水準之上，並聽說在目前服務的單位，受到很高的評價。

　　和大家一樣，他也有幾個所謂的「缺點」。我認為當他在處理工作中所遇到的挫折時，有必要多學習一些耐性，另外我想他也需要抑制一下他「過度」的幽默感。

　　然而，我必須說，此類的缺點，毫無疑問地可以用我所提到的優點來補足，故在此我毫無猶豫地推薦他應徵貴公司的職務。

　　貴公司若對順司還有任何其他疑問，我將很樂意一一為您答覆。

謹上

【語句注釋】◆ in support of ～ 「支持～」。◆ application for position 「工作的應徵」。position「職務，職位」。have a position in a bank「在銀行工作」。◆ be highly motivated to ～ 「對～很有熱誠，對～充滿雄心」。◆ succeed 「成就，達成」。◆ be well thought of 「受到很高的評價」。◆ what might be called 「所謂的」(= what is called)。◆ deal with 「應付，處理」。◆ setbacks 「挫折，失敗」。◆ temper 「抑制，緩和」。◆ I must say that ～ 「我必須說～」。口語中 I must say 置於開頭、句中或結尾時，指「真的～，完全～」的意思。◆ be outweighed by ～ 「可以～補足而綽綽有餘」。outweighed ～「比～還重，比～還多」The advantages outweigh the drawbacks 瑕不掩瑜）。

10

實　務

因下星期預定到貴地，希望能會面，以介紹新產品。此產品可說是劃時代的新商品，年底正式公開時，勢必造成轟動。因此在公開之前，希望務必向貴公司介紹等內容的信。

Dear Mr. Ambrose,

I shall be in Drewfield next week, and would appreciate an opportunity to visit you at your convenience and tell you about the exciting new line of pet cosmetics my company has imported from Japan.

These cosmetics are, to put it mildly, revolutionary, and promise to create a sensation in the pet care industry when they are officially released later this year.

If I may, I'd like to phone you on Monday, and arrange a suitable time to visit.

Yours faithfully,

安布羅斯先生台鑒:

　　我將在下星期到訪杜魯菲爾德，屆時若能有機會在您方便的時間，拜訪您並且報告有關本公司由日本進口、令人期待的新系列寵物美容用品，甚感是幸。

　　這些美容用品，即便保守的說，也可謂是革命性的新產品，預計在年底正式發售之後，勢必在寵物美容界，引發一陣熱潮。

　　可以的話，我將於星期一打電話給您，安排方便會面的時間。

謹上

【語句注釋】◆ at your convenience 「在您方便的時間」。另也有 at your earliest convenience 的說法。在希望對方及早回覆的情況下，若直言「敬請儘速回覆」的話，略嫌失禮，使用此表現，則較委婉。◆ a new line of products 「新系列的產品」。line「一系列（種類上雖屬同類的物品，但在大小、價錢、品質以及設計等方面略有不同的同系列產品）」。the spring line「春裝系列（服飾、配件等）」。◆ to put it mildly 「保守地說」。◆ revolutionary 「革命性的」。◆ promise to 「預計～，有希望～」。◆ create a sensation 「引發一陣熱潮」。◆ be released 「正式發售」。

雖然負責該區域的代表已回國，本地區也將移轉到其他區域管轄，然而為了在服務方面，不造成客戶的困擾，已建立起一如往常的高水準的服務體系，故敬請安心。

Dear Mr. Smith,

As you may know, Tommy Matsumoto, our representative in Cedar Falls, has returned to Japan, and responsibility for your area has been transferred to the Evansville regional office.

Please rest assured that the closure of the Cedar Falls office will in no way mean a lowering of the high standard of personal service we have always provided our valued customers. One of our highly-trained office staff will still be only a phone call away, and we have arranged for a representative to call on you at least once a month.

If you have any queries about the reorganization of our customer support presence in your area, please do not hesitate to call me directly.

Yours faithfully,

史密斯先生台鑒：

　　如您所知，本公司在希達佛爾斯的區域代表——湯米‧松本，已返回日本，而且貴區域的責任劃分也已移交伊凡斯維爾區域辦事處管理。

　　雖然希達佛爾斯辦事處已關閉，但是這絕不表示，我們到目前為止對本公司的重要顧客所提供的高水準的貼心服務，將因此而低落，故敬請安心。只要一通電話，我們受過高度訓練的工作人員，將隨時候教。此外，我們也安排了代表，至少每個月拜訪貴公司一次。

　　若您對貴區域中本公司的顧客支援體制的重組有任何疑問，請別猶豫，直接打電話給我。

謹上

【語句注釋】◆ **Please rest assured that ～** 「請對～感到安心」。◆ **in no ways** 「絕不～」。口語中，也經常使用 No ways!「可不可以請你加班?」「No ways!（休想!）」。◆ **our valued customers** 「本公司的重要顧客」。◆ **will be only a phone call away** 「只要一通電話，馬上回應客人的要求」。◆ **queries** 「疑問，質問」。比 question 還要正式的詞。◆ **customer support presence** 「顧客支援體制（的存在）」。presence 指「存在」。與 reorganization 共用時，則指「體制的組織更動」。◆ **please do not hesitate to ～** 「請別猶豫～」。

10–3 獎勵銷售的計畫

關於暑期獎勵銷售的年度計畫，特別針對該以什麼作為獎賞一事，詢問
現場人員意見的一封信。

Dear Mr. Craddock,

March is almost upon us, and once again it's time to think about our
Summer Sales Incentive Program.

As you know, this Program was introduced five years ago, and has been
an outstanding hit with our sales personnel throughout the United States.
The facts speak for themselves: the Program has been responsible for a
15–20% rise in overall sales during the otherwise slack summer months.

Not resting content with these encouraging figures, we here at Head
Office intend to expand the Program even further, and make it an even
more resounding success. To do this, what we need above all is feedback
from our local branches. We need to know what our front-line sales staff
think about the prizes we have offered so far, and what kind of prizes
they think we should offer in the future.

This is why I am writing to you and all our other branch managers. If you
have any comments, ideas, or suggestions about our Program, I want to
hear them. And if you have any criticisms of the Program, I want to hear
them too!

Yours,

克瑞達科先生台鑒：

　　3月份已近，又到了我們思考有關暑期獎勵銷售計畫的時候。

　　如您所知，此計畫在 5 年前開始實施，已在全美的推銷員之間，收到了驚人的成效。事實顯示此計畫的實施，提高了通常為淡季的夏天銷售總額的百分之十五到二十。

　　在此我們總公司不以這振奮人心的數字而滿足，並正考慮將此計畫更加擴展，使之邁向更輝煌的成功。為達到此目標，最需要知道的是，由各分店所反映的意見。我們必須聽取最前線的銷售人員，對至今提供的獎賞的看法，以及他們認為我們需要在未來提供什麼樣的獎勵。

　　這也是我提筆書寫此信給您和所有其他分店的經理的原因。若您對此計畫，有任何意見、辦法或建議，請讓我知道。甚至，若您對計畫有任何批評，也請不吝賜教。

謹上

【語句注釋】◆ incentive 「獎勵；給予動機」。◆ hit 「成功，一炮而紅」。◆ speak for oneself 「事實證明，闡明」。◆ has been responsible for ～ 「乃為～的原因；對～有益」。用以表示好事的原因時，也使用 responsible。◆ otherwise 「否則」。此指「若沒有實施此計畫的話～」。◆ Not resting content with ～ 「不以～為滿足」。其意與 We are not (do not rest) content with ～, and we intend to ～大致相同。◆ To do this 「為了做此事」。在此指「為了使此計畫更加成功」之意。◆ feedback 「反映的意見，回應」。◆ front-line 「最前線的」。front line（最前線）本為名詞，以連字號 (-) 連結之後，變成形容詞。◆ so far 「至今，到目前」。◆ This is why 「因此，所以」。直譯為「這就是～的原因」。內容指「因為想聽取意見，故書寫本信」之意。

　　向飛機上認識的人士，請求介紹韓國方面的生意對象。同時，並表達可
能的話，也可和對方在生意上有所合作的一封信。

Dear Mr. Chin,

It was indeed a pleasure to make your acquaintance on the flight from Seattle to Tokyo last Thursday. I enjoyed talking to you very much, and hearing about your business activities in Korea.

For some time now, my company has been considering expanding into the Korean market, but has held back for want of reliable business associates in that country.

We are a long-established company with a strong record of sales in several foreign countries, and have no wish to rush into a new market without first cementing firm ties with trustworthy business associates based in that market. At the moment our top priority is finding such trustworthy business associates, and discussing our proposals with them.

If you know of any companies that you think might be interested in doing business with us, I would truly appreciate your letting me know their names and, if possible, the names of persons to contact in those companies.

And if you yourself should be interested in exploring the possibility of a business arrangement with us, I would be prepared to fly to Seoul at any time suitable for you, and discuss this matter in person.

Yours sincerely,

金先生惠鑒：

　　上週四非常榮幸地在西雅圖到東京的飛機上，與您結緣相識。也非常高興的聽您談及有關您在韓國方面的生意情形。
到目前為止，本公司已考慮拓展韓國市場有一段時間了，然而卻因在韓國找不到值得信賴的生意夥伴而延宕。

　　本公司乃一在許多海外國家具有堅強的實際銷售成績的老字號，所以並不希望，在還沒有與當地值得信賴的生意對象，建立起堅實的關係之前，貿然進入新市場。我們目前的首要重點，在於找到如上述的可靠生意夥伴，進而與之協議本公司的計畫。

　　若您認為有哪些公司可能有興趣與我們合作，來信告訴我他們的公司名稱，若可能的話，以及聯絡人的姓名，我將非常的感激您。

　　此外，若您對與本公司合作的可能性有興趣的話，我將親自飛往漢城，在您方便的時間，討論相關事宜。

謹上

【語句注釋】◆ make your acquaintance 「與您結識」。◆ I enjoyed talking to you 「很高興和您談話」。enjoy 後面接動名詞 (～ing)，不接不定詞。◆ For some time now 「至今已有一段時間，已經過一陣子」。◆ hold back 「延緩決定」。◆ want 「缺乏」。和 lack 大致上意思相同。◆ long-established company 「歷史悠久的，老字號的」。◆ rush into ～ 「闖入～」。◆ based in ～ 「據點在～」。指 business associates that are based in ～的意思。◆ do business with 「和～作生意」。與 deal with 相同。◆ explore 「探尋，探求」。◆ arrangement 「約定」。

此為負責處理商標權糾紛的代理人，寄給委託人的顧問律師的一封信。因代理人聽說取得商標正式授權的日本公司的負責人與正在訴訟中的對方公司的人員見面，且向對方批評自己，對此表示抗議的信（請參照範例 10−6【參考】）。

Dear Mr. Wallis,

It has come to my attention that both Mr. Abe and Mr. Takeshita have **been in contact with** Mr. Kitazawa of Evergreen Trading, and have expressed strong **reservations** about my **handling** of the current dispute between Evergreen and your company.

I am deeply disturbed that two of your **licensees** here in Japan should have made such comments to Mr. Kitazawa, and am shocked to hear that they have **questioned** my professional judgment.

This is an intolerable situation, and unless it is resolved immediately, I shall **be forced to** resign my position of **trademark attorney** for your company.

Yours faithfully,

渥利斯先生台鑒:

　　獲悉阿部與竹下二位先生，曾與長春貿易的北澤先生接觸，並對此次長春貿易與貴公司之間的糾紛，表達了對本人的作法強烈的保留態度。

　　本人對取得貴公司日本授權的二位人士，向北澤先生提出如是批評一事，深以為擾。並驚愕地聽聞此二位對本人的專業判斷力，提出質疑。

　　此乃無法容忍之情況，若不馬上解決，本人勢必將辭去負責貴公司的商標權代理人一職。

　　　　　　　　　　　　　　　　　　　　　　　　　　　謹上

【語句注釋】◆ be in contact with ～　「與～接觸」。◆ reservation　「懷疑」。◆ handle　「處理」。◆ licensee　「被授權的人」。「給予許可的人」則為 licensor, licenser。◆ question　「提出質疑，存有異議」。◆ be forced to ～　「必須～」。◆ trademark attorney　「商標權代理人」。通常商標權代理人，總稱為 a patent attorney。但是，正確地來說，patent（專利權）這個字，因含有「著作權、商標權、發明權」等，故有時也分別稱之為 a trademark attorney 或 a design attorney 等。在美國，商標權代理人稱為 a patent attorney，然而在英國則稱作 a patent agent。順便一提，「律師」在美國稱作 attorney，英國則稱為 lawyer。通常律師名片上的職銜多採美國式，譯為 attorney。

範例 10-5 的回函。表示非常信賴對方，希望今後還能繼續合作的一封信。

Dear Mr. Haraguchi,

I was terribly concerned when I received your fax of March 24. Please let me make clear that I **hold you in the highest esteem** as a professional. The work that you have done for us has been of the very best quality.

I hold the same view of Mr. Abe and Mr. Takeshita and do **not** believe that they would **in any way unwittingly** say anything that would be harmful to your reputation. If your concern arises out of anything you heard from Mr. Kitazawa, in my opinion, there is nothing Mr. Kitazawa says that should **be given any credence**. I have been handling commercial litigation for over 30 years as an attorney, and I have never in my experience **encountered** anyone quite as **malicious** as Mr. Kitazawa.

There is **a body of English literature devoted to** the quotation "hell hath **no fury like a woman scorned**". These stories describe a mad **scorned** woman who plots to **get even with** the man who scorned her by destroying his reputation, and the reputations of his friends and relations. Mr. Kitazawa's actions fit this mold.

His letter to all of the officers and directors of Riverbank **vilifying** me has me upset. I can well imagine how disturbed you are about his actions toward you. However, I know you, Mr. Abe, and Mr. Takeshita to be men of good will and I so regard myself. Therefore, let us all stick together and the **truth will out**.

I would be most upset to lose you as our trademark attorney, and I trust that we can work together for many years.

Kindest personal regards,

原口先生台鑒：

　　收到您 3 月 24 日所發的傳真，我深感擔憂。在此鄭重的聲明，我對您為法律專家之素養，予以最高的評價。過去您為本公司所提供的服務，在品質上也至為傑出。

　　我對阿部與竹下二位先生，也抱持著相同的看法，絕不相信他們會在無意識中說出任何傷及您聲譽的言語。若您是因為聽了北澤先生的話，而如此擔心的話，在我看來，北澤先生的言論完全沒有任何信用可言。我以律師身分，處理商業訴訟超過 30 年以上，在我的經驗之中，從沒遇過像北澤先生一樣心存惡意的人。

　　在英國有以諺語「地獄並不比被拋棄的女人可怕」為主題的文學作品。這些作品中，描寫著遭受拋棄而導致瘋狂的女子，為了向拋棄自己的男子報仇，用盡各種手段破壞他及其朋友、親人之聲譽。北澤先生的行為，正與此類角色不謀而合。

　　本人曾因他寄給「大河銀行」職員和董事們的一封中傷信而十分惱怒。我完全可以想像您對他待您的行徑有多麼困擾。然而，我知道您、阿部先生及竹下先生，都是心存善意的人，並相信自己也是。因此，我們應該團結一致，澄清事實真相。

　　若本公司失去了您作為負責商標權的代理人，本人將感到深為痛惜。我深信我們來日方長，一定可以繼續合作下去的。

謹上

【語句釋義】 ◆ hold (a person) in high esteem 「對（人）大為尊敬」。◆ not in any way 「絕對不～」。在此，I do not believe that they would in any way unwittingly say ～ 的表現，可視作 I believe that would not say in any way。◆ unwittingly 「漫不經心，無意識地，不留意地」。◆ give credence to ～ 「信任～」。◆ encounter 「遭遇，碰見」。encounter with the unknown「與未知的邂逅」。◆ malicious 「有惡意（敵意）的，壞心眼的」。◆ a body of English literature 「英國文學作品」。body 指「（文書等的）本文，主體」。在此解釋為「作品，著作」的意思。◆ devoted to ～ 「以～為主題，採取～為主題」。◆ "Hell hath no fury like a woman scorned". 《諺語》「地獄也沒有像被輕視的女人，這麼可怕」。換句話說，就是「被拋棄的女人，極端可怕」的意思。◆ scorn 「輕視，蔑視」。plot and connive at「策略（謀略，詭計）。◆ get even with ～ 「向～報復」。◆ vilify 「中傷」。◆ Truth will out 《諺語》「真相大白」。

【參考】範例 10–5 及 10–6 的往返書信，內容多少有些複雜，在此加以如下之說明。

範例 10–6 的本信的發信人渥利斯先生 (Mr. Wallis)，乃為發生糾紛之商標的商標權所有者——美國廠商（A 公司）的顧問律師。此外，本信的收信人，即範例 10–5 的發信人原口先生，則為負責 A 公司在日本的商標權代理人。

另一方面，A 公司賦予了日本廠商（B 公司）自己公司之商標權的使用授權。因此，B 公司則為 A 公司的授權廠商 (licensee)。阿部與竹下二位先生，則是此 B 公司的職員。此外，被認為是侵犯商標權，製造了此次糾紛的公司為長青公司。因而從中作梗的，則為長春公司方面的代理人北澤先生。

原口先生因居心不良的北澤先生的計謀，而怒氣沖沖的揚言辭去擔任代理人的職務。為了安撫勃然大怒的原口先生，渥利斯先生因而書寫了此封真誠流露的長信。讓人感受到委託人對於代理人的誠意與信賴，實值得參考。

有意拓展日本市場的外國設計公司所寄出的一封信，旨在介紹該公司及尋找海外合作契機。

Dear Mr. Sullivan,

Perhaps you remember me from the Solena Incorporated Christmas Party last month, at which I had the pleasure of exchanging business cards with you.

I was able to speak with you for only a few minutes at that time, and I would like to take this opportunity to tell you a little more about my company and myself.

Nagaoka Design was founded in 1986, and in only a few short years has grown into one of the largest and most successful design bureaus in Japan. Among our clients we are proud to number some of the biggest names in Japanese industry, and many of our industrial designs have won awards both in this country and abroad.

I joined Nagaoka Design five years ago, and at present I am the chief of the Market Research Section.

During our brief chat at the party, you mentioned that your company is considering introducing a new line of kitchen utensils into Japan. As I am sure you are aware, each market is different, as are the needs of local consumers.

Product localization to meet the unique needs of the Japanese market is one of the specialties of Nagaoka Design, and if there is any way that we

---

can be of assistance to your company, I should be delighted to visit your office and explain in detail the many services we offer.

In the meantime, I have **taken the liberty of enclosing** an illustrated **portfolio** of some of the design projects we have undertaken in the last few years.

Yours sincerely,

蘇利文先生台鑒:

　　或許您還記得，我在上個月索林納公司的聖誕節派對中，曾極榮幸地與您交換過名片。

　　在當時，只能和您寥談數語。希望藉書寫此信的機會，願向您報告較多有關本人及公司的情況。

　　本公司長岡設計創立於 1986 年，並在短短的幾年之間，快速地成長為日本最大也最成功的設計公司。在本公司的客戶中，我們很驕傲的擁有許多代表日本產業界的知名人物。此外，本公司的工業設計也榮獲過海內外的許多獎項。

　　本人於 5 年前加入長岡設計公司，目前擔任市場調查部部長。

　　在聖誕派對上的簡短談話中，您提到貴公司正在考慮介紹一系列的廚房用品到日本。也相信您了解各地市場屬性不同，以及當地消費者的需求也迥異。

　　將產品本土化以迎合日本市場的獨特需求，為長岡設計最擅長的範疇之一。若有任何我們能夠協助貴公司的地方，我將很樂意地造訪貴公司，向您說明我們所提供的服務。

　　在此擅自附上本公司過去數年間經手的設計企畫案中的幾份附圖的資料，敬請見諒。

　　　　　　　　　　　　　　　　　　　　　　　　　　　　　　謹上

【語句注釋】◆ **I had the pleasure of exchanging business cards** 「很榮幸地與您交換名片」。I exchanged business cards 在意義上也相同，只是如本範例的寫法，可看出自己向對方表示的敬意，感覺上較好些。◆ **I would like to take this opportunity to～** 「想利用此機會～」。在此句子中，不用 chance，而用 opportunity。◆ **found** 「創設」。與 establish 大體上相同。◆ **bureau** 「組織」。與 organization 大致上相同，在此範例中指「公司」之意。◆ **I joined Nagaoka Design** 「加入長岡設計公司」。通常不說 I entered ～。◆ **～ is considering introducing** 「考慮介紹」。consider 後面接動名詞 (～ing)，不接不定詞，consider to introduce 為錯誤用法。◆ **line** 「一系列的商品」。◆ **as are the needs** 「需求方面也相同」。將 as the needs of local consumers are different 中的 different 省略，形成倒裝子句。◆ **localization** 「本土化」。◆ **specialty** 「專門，專攻範疇」。◆ **take the liberty of enclosing** 「很抱歉，在此擅自附上～」。單以 I am enclosing, I enclose, 或 I have enclosed 表現，在意義上也相同，不過因為對方並沒有要求，而是自己決定附上的，所以在禮貌上先說聲抱歉。◆ **portfolio** 「企畫案」。

針對某契約問題懸而未決的狀態，希望對方照著該公司新富先生所言，早早解決問題為主旨的信。

Dear Mr. Amano,

I have received a letter from Mr. Shintomi telling me that the matter of the Trivet contract should have been **concluded** sometime ago. I must say that I agree with Mr. Shintomi. As you know, Merrivale's relationship with Concorde is **defined** by contract and Mr. Shintomi is clearly **within his rights** in being critical of the lack of a conclusion of this matter.

Mr. Amano, I believe you and I are both **positive** persons. I am doubly distressed by this dispute because it is **negative** for all concerned: Mr. Shintomi, you, Mr. Okada, myself and our companies. There are many positive things we can do with the Merrivale brand name. Let's conclude this matter and **move on to** something positive.

Very truly yours,

天野先生台鑒：

　　我已收到新富先生的來信，告知有關特利維特契約的事情，應早在日前有所解決。我得在此聲明，本人同意新富先生的看法。如您所知，梅利維爾與康克爾德二公司的關係，均在契約中規定得很清楚。新富先生對本事件的懸而未決提出批評，很明顯地並不逾越他分內的權限範圍。

　　天野先生，本人相信您和我都是很積極的人。我為此糾紛陷入雙重的困擾中。原因在於，此紛爭對新富先生、您、岡田先生、我本人以及我們的公司，都有負面的影響。而本人認為，梅利維爾的品牌，應可使我們推動許多正面價值的事業才是。讓我們及早結束此一紛爭，朝向更為正面積極的事業吧！

謹上

【語句注釋】◆ conclude 「結尾，使終結」。但是 conclude a contract 等，以「契約、協定、條約」等詞為受詞的場合，conclude 則成為「締結，連結」的意思。◆ define 「清楚規定」。◆ within one's rights 「自己的權限內」。◆ positive 「積極的，正面的」。◆ negative 「消極的，反面的」。◆ move on to 「移向～，向～轉移」。

雖新聞報導的內容本身，以公正的態度分析了整個事件，但是標題為了達到吸引讀者的目的，使用情緒化並帶有暗示負面內容的字眼，關於此點，向報社提出抗議的信。

Dear Sir,

I wirte in reference to the article headlined "Watch Out, Here Come the Samurai" that appeared in the September 26th edition of your newspaper.

Although the article as a whole is, I believe, a fair analysis of some of the problems that have accompanied the construction of our new production facility on the outskirts of New Malden, I regret the rather sensational and negative tenor of the headline.

I can assure you that over ninety percent of the labor force at the new facility has been recruited locally, and that none of the Japanese technicians or managers who will be arriving next month is either a "samurai" or, for that matter, has any warlike intentions whatever.

"Friendly Neighbors" has always been the Manabe Electrical Industries motto, and we have always placed the utmost emphasis on good relationships with the communities in which our plants are located.

I respectfully ask you to bear this in mind if you ever consider carrying another article about our plant.

Yours faithfully,

敬啟者:

　　我寫這封信，是關於貴報社在 9 月 26 日刊載以「小心！日本武士來了！」為標題的新聞。

　　對於本公司在新摩爾登的郊外，建設新生產設施時所伴隨發生的幾點問題，您的報導，本人認為，就整體上作了公正的分析。然而，卻對相當情緒化且帶有負面含義的標題，感到遺憾。

　　在此可以斷然向您保證的是，此新設施中百分之九十以上的勞動力，全在當地聘僱。而且，下個月將抵達的日籍技術人員或管理人員等，既非「日本武士」，也沒有人持有任何「好戰」的意圖。

　　「友好近鄰」一直是真鍋電氣工業的座右銘。我們也總是最為注重與當地社區維持親善的關係。

　　今後若您考慮刊載有關本公司的其他報導時，請您銘記以上所述為荷。

謹上

【語句注釋】◆ in reference to ～　「關於～」。◆ article headlined ～　「以～為標題的文章（報導）」。◆ accompany　「伴隨～而發生」。◆ production facilities　「生產設施」。◆ outskirts　「郊外，郊區」。◆ tenor　「要旨，大意」。◆ labor force　「勞動力 (= work force)」。◆ recruit　「新進，補充」。◆ for that matter　「實際，順便一提，就此而言」。◆ warlike　「好戰的」。◆ communities　「社區，社區裏的人們」。

針對出貨日期不知對方是否誤解一事，加以說明的一封信。

Dear Mr. Goldstein,

This morning I briefed Mr. Hamaguchi, the Head of Overseas Operations at Takasaki Manufacturing, on the substance of the meeting I had with you last week.

When I told him that you expected shipment of heavy-duty hydraulic jacks to begin in early December, he expressed puzzlement over this, and asked me to write to you for clarification.

The fact is that our main plant in Takasaki will not be in a position to ship such items until March at the very earliest. Our office has never, to his knowledge, promised such early shipment.

I am sorry to trouble you with this matter, but could I ask you to let me know the basis for your expectation?

Yours truly,

哥德斯汀先生台鑒：

　　今天早晨，本人已對高崎工業的國際事業部部長浜口先生簡要地說明了上週與您會面時所作的談話。

　　當我告訴他，您預計大型油壓起重機的出貨將在 12 月初開始時，他表示相當困惑，並要我寫信給您，以查明此點。

　　實際上，在高崎的總廠方面，最快也要到明年 3 月份，才有可能裝船出貨。在浜口先生的記憶中，本公司並不曾允諾您如此早的出貨。

　　很抱歉因此事打擾您，但可否告知我方，您是根據什麼而有此預期的。

謹上

獲知裝船日期將比原先的約定大幅延緩（範例 10-10），陳訴對方若不改善，將就此斷絕生意往來的信。

Dear Mr. Serizawa,

Before coming to your query about the shipment of heavy-duty jacks, let me just say how much I enjoyed my meeting with you in Tokyo. I find it very irritating, and not a little counter-productive, to have to talk through an interpreter. It made such a change being able to talk one-on-one with such a fluent speaker of English as yourself.

Yes, you are correct, I did say that I expected shipment of heavy-duty hydraulic jacks in early December. This was the date given to me by Yoshi Yamamoto, your representative here in Iowa.

I was shocked and disturbed to hear that you will not be able to ship until next March. This scheduling is completely unacceptable, and I shall have to consider making other arrangements.

Although I have enjoyed doing business with your company in the past, I have to tell you now that unless I hear from you within one week with a more realistic shipping schedule, I shall consider our business relationship to be at an end.

Yours faithfully,

芹澤先生台鑒：

　　在沒進入您問及的有關大型起重機裝船出貨的正題之前，在此先向您說聲，我非常的高興與您在東京相會。藉由翻譯人員的談話，總覺得有如隔靴搔癢，甚至有些反效果。而此回能直接與您這般英文流暢的人，做一對一的面談，實有完全不同的感受。

　　是的，您所言正確。我確實提及我期待 12 月初貴公司的大型油壓起重機的裝船出貨。而這是貴公司在愛荷華的代表，山本吉先生給我的日期。

　　聽到貴公司一直要到明年 3 月才可能裝船出貨，深感震驚與困擾。我們完全無法接受這樣的預定行程，並且正考慮作其他安排。

　　雖然過去我們一直與貴公司合作得很愉快，不過在此必須告知您的是，除非貴公司能在一星期內提出較為實際的出貨預定行程，否則我將考慮就此斷絕與貴公司之間的生意往來關係。

謹上

【語句注釋】◆ I find it very irritating to ～　「對～感到焦慮」。irritating 本為「焦慮不安」的形容詞，此時用作「隔靴搔癢」之意。「find + 受詞 + 受詞補語」的句型中，it 為假的受詞，真正的受詞為 to 之後的句子。◆ not a little counter-productive　「相當的反效果」。not a little 和 very 意義大致上相同，但更具強調的意味。◆ it made such a change being able to talk　「能夠彼此對談，感覺有很大的不同」。it 在此處為虛主詞，真正的主詞為 being 之後的句子。◆ representative　「職員，駐外代表」。representative 指代表（代理）某人或某組織的人，但通常不用於經理級以上人員，多為一般公司職員（特別是業務員）。◆ disturb　「使～不安」。◆ ship　「出貨」。後面本應加上 the jacks 或 the goods 等，但當可以從前後文判斷文意時，多省略受詞。◆ consider making other arrangements　「考慮其他的安排」。在此指的是「取消向貴公司的訂單，而考慮向其他公司訂貨」。注意不可用 consider to make。◆ unless I hear from you　「若貴公司沒有聯絡的話」。比 if I do not hear from you 強硬的用法。

因駐外代表的錯誤，而無法遵守出貨的約定，就此說明並為之道歉的信。

Dear Mr. Goldstein,

Mr. Hamaguchi has asked me to write to you **on his behalf**, to offer an explanation for the unfortunate misunderstanding that **seems to have arisen over** the shipping schedule of the hydraulic jacks your company ordered in September.

Production of the **new line** of heavy-duty hydraulic jacks was **conditional upon** completion of additional floor space at our Takasaki plant, and the installation of new **machinery**. This completion and installation were originally scheduled for late October, and it is likely that Mr. Yamamoto's optimistic estimate was based on this timing.

By early October it was clear, however, that work on the new floor space **was well behind schedule**, and a memo **to that effect** was sent to all our offices in both Japan and other countries. Mr. Yamamoto should have been aware of this memo, and **should not have promised** December shipment. Please accept our profoundest apologies for his **unwarranted** action.

Although we cannot possibly **bring** the shipping date further **forward** than the beginning of March, in consideration of the responsibility we feel for the trouble caused by the delay, we are prepared to let you have the original order of fifty units **at cost**, and are prepared to cover shipment and insurance.

We hope this offer is acceptable, and that we can continue to do business in the future.

Yours truly,

哥德斯汀先生台鑒：

　　本人受浜口先生的請託，代表他向您致上此信，關於貴公司於 9 月份訂購的油壓式起重機的出貨預定行程，產生令人遺憾的誤會，做一說明。

　　新機種大型起重機的製造與本公司高崎工廠的樓層面積擴張的完成，以及新機械設備的裝設密切相關。本來擴張的完成和裝設完工均預定在 10 月底，山本先生樂觀的預測也許就是根據此原訂計畫的吧！

　　然而到了 10 月初，我們才清楚地了解到，樓層面積擴大的作業比預定計畫嚴重落後。因此，我們即刻向國內外辦事處發佈有關的通知。山本先生應該有接獲此通知，實不該對您承諾 12 月出貨。在此對山本先生未盡責的行為，致上最深的歉意。

　　雖然我們無法將裝船出貨的日期，提早到 3 月初之前，但考慮到須對因延遲而對您造成的困擾負責，我們決定以原價提供您原先所訂購的 50 臺機器，而運費及保險費用，均由本公司負擔。

　　我們希望您能接受此一提議，並期待今後也能繼續地保持合作。

謹上

【語句注釋】◆ on his behalf 「代替他，代表他」。◆ seem to have arisen over～「似乎起因於～」。arisen 為 arise 的過去分詞。與 occurred 大致上相同。在此句中的 over 指「有關於～」之意。與 about 大致上也相同。◆ new line 「新（商品的）機種」。◆ conditional upon 「以～為條件、全憑～」。upon 也可用 on 代替。◆ machinery 「（集合名詞）機械」。◆ was well behind schedule 「比原定計畫落後許多」。相反的「比原定計畫提早」則為 be ahead of schedule。「照計畫」則為 be on schedule。此處，well 指「相當，非常」之意。與 far 大致上相同。◆ to that effect 「那樣的意思」。◆ should not have promised 「不應該承諾～」。◆ unwarranted 「不當的」。◆ bring ～ forward 「提前，提早」。◆ at cost 「以原價」。

204

11

遷移通知以及其他

向有業務往來的公司，通知辦公室遷移的書信。

Dear Sirs,

We are pleased to inform you that our current offices will be relocated to the following address.

We look forward to your continuing patronage and support in the future.

> Diamond Building 35F
> Hongo 4-1, Shirazaki City
> Kanagawa Pref.
> 243 Japan

The telephone and fax numbers will remain the same.

Sincerely,

敬啟者：

　　我們現在的辦公室，已遷移到如下新址，特此敬告通知。
　　並期待您未來繼續的愛顧與支持。
　　日本國神奈川縣白崎市本鄉四丁目一番地
　　鑽石大樓 35 樓
　　郵遞區號 243
　　電話及傳真號碼仍然相同。

謹上

【語句注釋】◆ **We are pleased to inform you that**　「在此敬告通知～」。此為書寫通知信函時的慣用句型，其他還有如下的例句。(1) We have the pleasure of informing you that ～ (2) It is our pleasure to inform you that ～ (3) We would like to inform you that ～ (4) This is to inform you that ～ 等等。◆ **our current office**　「本公司現在的辦公室」。◆ **be located**　「遷移」。◆ **your continuing patronage and support**　「敬請貴公司繼續愛顧與支持」。

【注意】撰寫此類通知時，通常新住址上不附加公司名。公司名一般放在信的開頭。

隨著新辦公室的落成，在小型的啟用儀式之後將有個輕鬆的自助式餐會。有關的詳細情形，下星期祕書將與之聯絡，在此先簡單地通知，敬請務必參加的邀請函。

Dear Ms. Tsubouchi,

Our new office in central Takasaki will be completed next month, and the work of relocation should take about a week.

We plan to hold a small opening ceremony at 10:00 am on Tuesday, April 17, to be followed by an informal buffet-style reception for all our closest clients and business associates.

We would be honored if you could come to both the opening ceremony and the reception. My secretary will contact you next week, and will send you more details of the location of our new office if you require them.

Yours sincerely,

坪內小姐惠鑒:

　　本公司設於高崎市市中心的新辦公室,將於下個月落成完工。遷移的作業,預計花 1 個禮拜的時間。

　　我們計畫在 4 月 17 日,星期二,上午 10 點,舉行一小型的落成典禮,隨後並將有個非正式的自助餐會以宴請我們的老顧客及生意上有往來的人士。

　　若您能蒞臨開幕典禮暨餐會,我們將感到無上光榮。本人的祕書將在下個禮拜與您聯繫,若您需要的話,也將寄給您一份附有新辦公室詳細地圖的資料。

謹上

語句注釋】◆ work of relocation 　「遷移的作業」。relocate 中含有「安置在新場所,~轉移」之意。◆ hold a small opening ceremony 　「舉行一小型的開幕典禮」。◆ to followed by an informal reception 　「隨後將舉行一非正式的餐會」。◆ closest ents and business associates 　「熟客及生意上的夥伴」。◆ We would be honored if u could ～ 　「若貴公司～,本公司將感到無上光榮」。◆ will contact you next week 子於下星期與您聯繫」。◆ more details of the location 　「有關地點更加詳細的情形」。

11-2　新辦公室啟用典禮的邀請　209

因有急事聯絡，撥了名片上的電話號碼，卻已經是空號，而無法聯絡上。為了契約的事情，必須緊急地與之商量討論，故希望在接到信後，能儘快地與其聯絡等內容。

Dear Mr. Nabeshima,

I need to get in touch with you rather urgently about the Springfield contract, but find that the telephone number listed on your business card is no longer current. I have tried, and been unable, to find your new telephone number via directory inquiries.

I assume that you have moved your office, and hope that this letter will be forwarded to your new address.

Please call me as soon as you receive this letter. The matter needs to be dealt with as soon as possible, and it is important that I discuss it with you beforehand.

Sincerely,

鍋島先生台鑒:

　　有關斯普林菲爾德的契約，須緊急地與您商議，卻發現您名片上的電話號碼，已無法接通。我曾嘗試著詢問查號臺，卻也找不到您新的電話號碼。

　　我想貴辦公室可能已經遷移，希望這封信能被轉送到您的新址。

　　請您接到這封信後，儘速撥電話與我聯絡。本事件需要儘快解決，重要的是我得事先跟您商量討論。

謹上

【語句注釋】◆ get in touch with ～ 「與～聯絡 (= contact)」。◆ no longer current 「已不再使用」。current 另有「貨幣流通」的意思。◆ directory inquiries 「查號臺」(= directory assistance, directory information)。◆ be forwarded to ～ 「被轉送至～」。同樣的意思，雖也可使用 transferred，但此表現中，含有「（某人）被調職」的含意。◆ deal with 「處理」。

11-3　希望已搬遷的對方公司與之聯絡的請求　211

　　有人打電話到已調職者原來的工作地點，因對方身分不明，故未轉告其轉調後的詳細地點。之後，同一人又寄信過來，故在此轉送等內容的信。

Dear Tomio,

A few days ago my secretary Dorothy received a phone call from someone calling himself Taniguchi (I think I have the spelling right), asking to speak to you. When she told him that you had been transferred back to Osaka, he asked for your address and telephone number in Japan.

Dorothy tells me that his English was not too good, and she had a lot of trouble understanding him. Unsure of who he was, or why he wanted to contact you, she refused to give him the information he wanted, and asked him to write to you care of the Toronto office. I must say I think she made the right decision, but I do hope whatever he had to say was not urgent.

This morning we received a letter addressed to you. There is no sender or return address on the envelope, but I assume it is from the same Taniguchi who called earlier.

I am enclosing this letter unopened. Please let me know if it requires any action at this end.

Yours,

親愛的富雄：

　　數日前，我的祕書桃樂西接到一通自稱 Taniguchi（我想應該沒拼錯）的來電，並希望和您通話。當祕書轉告了您已調職回大阪後，對方要求告訴他，您在日本的住址及電話。

　　桃樂西告訴我，此人的英文不是很好，故相當難以理解他的話意。因不確定對方到底是誰，為何要與您聯絡，所以桃樂西拒絕告訴他他想要的資訊，並告訴他可以寫信到多倫多支店，再轉交給您。我認為桃樂西作了正確的決定，但希望此人沒有什麼急事須找您。

　　今天早上，我們收到了一封給您的信。信封上沒寫上任何發信人的姓名或住址，不過我猜想應是那位先前打過電話的 Taniguchi 先生。

　　在此附上此封未拆開的信，若您需要我們做什麼，請再聯絡。

謹上

【語句注釋】◆ **I have the spelling right**　「拼音拼得正確」。在此的 have 為「在～狀態之下」的不完全及物動詞。the spelling 為受詞，right 為受詞補語。◆ **be transferred**　「調職」。transfer 為「使～調職」之及物動詞。有時也以不及物動詞 I transfer 的形態表現。◆ **was not too good**　「不太好」。實際上是想說 was poor，但率直地說出，又嫌過於露骨、不客氣，故以此婉轉地表示。諸如此類的修辭，是非常重要的。◆ **Unsure of ～**「因對～不確定」。若以 Being Unsure of ～ 的形式來考慮，則很容易看出分詞片語的結構。◆ **～re of ～**　「由～轉交」。書寫收信人姓名時，經常寫成 c/o Mr. Taro Yamada 的形式。◆ **～turn address**　「寄信人住址；回信地址」。◆ **enclose this letter unopened**　「附上未封的此信」。unopened 和前面出現過的 unsure of 的用法相同，表示「呈未開封的狀態」附帶狀況。

聖誕節時收信人將不在自己的家，向第三者詢問其通訊地址的一封信。

Dear Ms. Simpkins,

I would like to send Mr. Gilbertson a Christmas card this year, but I understand he will be in Vancouver for most of December.

Would you happen to know his address in Vancouver? I thought of sending the card to his usual Boston address, but that would mean him getting it some time in January.

Perhaps it would have been quicker to contact him directly about this, but I wanted the card to be a surprise, and could think of no better person to ask than yourself.

Sincerely,

新普金斯小姐惠鑒：

　　我今年想寄聖誕卡片給吉柏特森先生，但據悉他 12 月份都將在溫哥華。

　　不知您是否知道他在溫哥華的住址？我雖也考慮過將卡片寄到他在波斯頓的老地址，不過，這麼作的話，他將到 1 月份才可能收到此信。

　　或許最快的方式是與他本人直接聯絡，但我希望讓他驚喜一下，所以，我想還是問您最好。

謹上

收到了對方贈送的年終禮物，但告知公司的原則，不能收受禮物的一封信。

Dear Mr. Chiba,

I am very grateful for your thoughtfulness and consideration in sending me such a generous year-end gift, but I am afraid that I am unable to accept it in either an official or a personal capacity.

Although I understand it is a custom in your country to send year-end gifts to people to whom the sender feels in some way obliged, my company has a firm policy about receiving gifts from clients.

Please let me take this opportunity to wish you a very Happy New Year.

Truly,

千葉先生台鑒:

　　承蒙您如此地關心與體貼，慷慨地致贈年終禮品，在此由衷地感謝。然而，於公於私，我恐怕都不能接受您的厚禮。

　　雖然我能了解，在年終佳節時致贈禮物給值得感謝的人們一舉，在貴國是個習慣，但本公司對收受顧客的贈禮，有著相當嚴格的規定。

　　並藉此機會，由衷地祝福您有個非常愉快的新年。

　　　　　　　　　　　　　　　　　　　　　　　　　　　　謹上

上回見面時，因英文名片已用完，故補寄給對方等的通知信函。

Dear Mr. Deane,

May I apologize once again for not being able to present you with one of my English-language business cards when we met at the press reception on Monday evening.

It was extremely embarrassing for me to discover that I had run out of English cards, and I did not want to offend you by scribbling my name and address on one of my Japanese cards.

Please accept the enclosed card with my sincerest apologies.

Yours truly,

迪恩先生台鑒：

　　星期一晚上在記者招待會上與您見面時，無法奉贈本人的英文名片，在此再度地表示歉意。

　　當時，很困窘地發現自己的英文名片正好用完，卻又不希望失禮地在日文名片上，草草書寫自己的姓名及住址代替。

　　請接受我由衷的歉意及隨函附上的名片。

　　　　　　　　　　　　　　　　　　　　　　　　　　　　謹上

【語句注釋】◆ business card 「業務用的名片」。◆ press reception 「記者招待會」。例如，為發表新產品，邀請傳播媒體工作人員的招待會。◆ embarrassing 「不巧；困窘」。◆ run out of 「（手邊持有的）正好用完」。run short of ～為「變少」。◆ offend 「使某人不高興、傷害某人的感情」。◆ scribble 「疾書，草草書寫」。◆ apology 「道歉，賠不是」。此時通常如上例以複數形 apologies 表示。

12

電子郵件、傳真

雖已登記入會，卻遲遲未收到會員資料，希望對方確認的電子郵件。

To: support@pixelpix.com
Subject: Enrollment

I visited your Web site last week, and registered for your special VIP Member's Room.

I haven't received a membership packet yet.

Could you please check up on this, and let me know what has happened?

Michiko Amemiya
micchan@st.kannet.or.jp

位址：support@pixelpix.com
主旨：註冊

　　我於上週造訪了貴公司的網站，並在特別 VIP 會員室，做了登錄。
至今卻尚未收到會員資料。
可否請您查一下，並告知目前狀況如何？

雨宮美智子
micchan@st.kannet.or.jp

【語句注釋】◆ To: support@pixelpix.com 「電子郵件位址 (= e-mail address)」。只要向伺服器的管理者提出申請，使用者就可以擁有自己的電子郵件位址。一個完整的位址包括：(1) support = 使用者代號（由小寫英文字母及數字組成）。(2) @ = at 的標誌。(3) com = （主要為美國）一般企業、公司。此外，也有的系統以 co + 國名（例如：co.uk）的方式取代 .com。臺灣採用 .com.tw。此封收信人位址中的～pixelpix.com 即伺服器的網址。◆ enrollment 「登記，註冊」。◆ visit 「上網站，進入網站」。◆ Web site 「網站」。web 「（蜘蛛網般的）資訊網路 (information network)」。◆ packet 「資料袋」。

回覆通知會員資料已經寄出，但尚須等候一些時日才能收到。此外，從新聞上得知日本遭受強颱侵襲，提醒對方多加小心。

To: micchan@st.kannet.or.jp
Subject: Re: Enrollment

>I haven't received a membership packet yet.

Hi there :)

Since we are mailing the package to Japan, it will take a bit longer than our normal two week processing. I see from the news that Japan has been hit by a big typhoon. Take care and stay dry! :)

Betty

位址：micchan@st. kannet.or.jp
主旨：回覆：註冊

>至今卻尚未收到會員資料。

您好 :)
　　我們已將資料袋寄去日本，可能會比我們正常的處理時間 2 個星期還要久一些。我從新聞報導上得知日本遭受強烈颱風侵襲，請小心別被風雨淋溼了。:)

貝蒂

語句注釋】◆ > I haven't received a membership packet yet. 出現於前一封郵件
範例 12-1）的一句話。在回覆上一封收到的電子郵件時，通常會重複對方郵件中的某個部
分用以對照。藉此，收到回信的一方，馬上就能理解對方所回覆的重點。◆ stay dry
別被風雨淋溼了」。dry 指「乾燥的」，stay 為「在～的狀態、保持～的樣子」。用法如 Stay
appy!「祝你幸福快樂！」等。◆ :) 「微笑標誌」。在冒號的後面加上右括弧而成。向左
專90 度，即可看出一個笑臉的形狀。

12-3 要求從電子郵件名單中除名

要求對方將自己的名字從電子郵件名單上刪除的信件。

To: listmanager@folkcraft.com
Subject: Unsubscribe from List

Could you please **remove** my name from your **mailing list**? I have enjoyed reading it very much, but I'm afraid I no longer have the time to **keep up with** the **message traffic**.

Nobuo Hamaguchi
nhama@tw.sunrise.co.jp

12-4 對要求除名的回覆

應讀者要求為其除名，但仍樂意提供諮詢服務的回覆信件。

To: nhama@tw.sunrise.co.jp
Subject: Re: Unsubscribe from List

I will be more than happy to **delete** you from our list. Of course we always regret losing an **avid reader** of FolkCraft Online. If you have any further questions regarding your cancellation please **feel free to** contact us. Thank you for your interest in FolkCraft Online.

Jennie Schwartz
Administrative Assistant

是否可以請您將我的名字從您的電子郵件名單上刪除？雖然我很喜歡閱讀您寄來的資訊，但我恐怕已不再有時間負荷如此龐大的信件量。

浜口伸夫

【語句釋義】◆ remove 「刪除」。◆ mailing list 「電子郵件名單」。◆ keep up with ～ 「（為了不落後）趕上～」。◆ message traffic 「（訊息的）傳達量」。traffic 「（交通、運輸、處理的）量」。

　　本公司將會把您的名字從名單上刪除。FolkCraft Online 對於讀者的取消訂閱深感遺憾。若您對此還有其他任何問題的話，請儘管與我們聯絡。感謝您對 FolkCraft Online 的關心。

【語句注釋】◆ delete 「刪除」。◆ avid reader 「熱心的讀者」。◆ feel free to ～ 「隨意地～，自由地～」。

　　與提供網路撥接服務業者之間因主機系統故障所產生的糾紛。使用者在諮詢未果以及未獲善意回應之下憤而要求取消帳號。

To: feedback@birdnet.com
Subject: Access Problems

I wrote to you on August 3, asking about the problem I was having with accessing your service.

I still haven't received a response from you, and I am still unable to log on to the host computer.

In spite of this, you continue to bill me the standard monthly usage fee. I find this most unsatisfactory, and ask you to cancel my account immediately.

I had heard good things about your service, and expected much better. But now I must say I am extremely disappointed in your lack of customer support.

Kenji Matsuda
km234@mars.planet.co.jp

我於 8 月 3 日寫信詢問有關自己在撥接貴公司的服務上所遭遇的問題。然而至今仍未收到您的回應,而且我依然無法連上你們的主機。

　　儘管如此,貴公司依然不斷地寄來帳單要我支付每月的基本撥接費用。我對此十分不滿,在此要求您立即取消我的帳號。

　　之前我聽說貴公司的服務頗佳,對你們寄予很高的期望,但現在我必須坦言,你們在顧客支援服務這一點上,實在令人感到非常失望。

松田健司

【語句注釋】◆ access 「靠近,接近」。此處則是指連接上線路。◆ log on 「開始使用 (= log in)」。指使用者將姓名或密碼等資料輸入電腦系統後,整個系統即可開始使用的手續。(log on/log in = To enter into a computer the information required to begin a session.) ◆ host computer 「電腦主機」。指可同時連接多數的終端機(個人電腦)並使其同時使用的電腦。host 中有「接受」以及「多數」的意義。◆ account 「帳號」。與網路撥接服務業者簽契約時,所給與的「使用者 ID」(與會員代號類似)和個人密碼(為了防止他人盜用使用者 ID 的暗號),二者合稱為 account。

替無法順利撥接上網的顧客處理與網路撥接服務業者之間契約中止的手續等內容的回覆。

To: km234@mars.planet.co.jp
Subject: Account Problems

Dear Kenji,

I am sorry that you are not able to get online. I wish that I could have helped you out. It has been awhile since you sent me mail and I have forgotten the problem that you were having. I will send your mail to a friend of mine in the billing department and have them close the account. If you have time please send me mail and let me know what the problem was that you were having and what you had tried to resolve the problem.

Thanks.

Bobbie
feedback@birdnet.com

親愛的健司：

　　很抱歉您無法連線，真希望自己能幫得上忙。因為收到您寄來的電子郵件已有一段時間，我也忘記了您所遇到的困難為何，所以我將寄一封電子郵件給我在繳費部門的朋友，請他們將帳號結清。您若有時間，請寄 mail 給我，好讓我了解您遇到的問題以及您所嘗試過的解決辦法。

謝謝您。

　　　　　　　　　　　　　　　　　　　　　　　　　　　　波比

【語句注釋】◆ get online 「搭上線，連線上網」。◆ help out 「幫助」。幫助 (help)
使脫出 (out) 困境。◆ awhile 「有一段時間」。大致上與 some time 的用法相同。本來應
是表示很短的期間，但在這裏依上下文的語意及情境應解釋為「相當長的一段期間」。◆
billing department 「繳費部門」。◆ have them close the account 「使他們結清帳
號」。也就是從帳號名單中除名。此時的 have 為「使～，讓～」的使役動詞，後加省略 to
的不定詞。◆ resolve 「解決」。亦可用 solve。

　　使用者對於網路撥接服務業者沒有處理自己的解約要求一事表示不滿，因而再度去函告知對方，若再不儘速解決，將訴之法律途徑。

To: feedback@birdnet.com
Subject: Re: Account Problems

On August 27 I sent you an email message asking you to **cancel my account forthwith**.

I was shocked to find that you have once again **billed** me for a service I have not received.

Not only do I insist you immediately refund the charge for October, I expect a confirmation from you that my account has, indeed, been closed.

If I do not receive such confirmation within 48 hours, I shall ask my lawyer for advice on this matter.

Kenji Matsuda
km234@mars.planet.co.jp

我於 8 月 27 日發了一封電子郵件，要求您即刻取消我的帳號。

　　然而，真是令我震驚，貴公司竟然又再次寄來我根本沒使用到的服務費帳單。

　　在此不但堅持貴公司必須立即退還給我 10 月份的月費，同時，也希望您能給我一個答覆，確認我的帳號已「確實地」被取消。

　　我若在 48 小時內未收到您確實的答覆，將逕與律師商討此事。

　　　　　　　　　　　　　　　　　　　　　　　　　　松田健司

【語句注釋】◆ cancel my account　「取消我的帳號」。也就是從繳費名單上除名的意思。◆ forthwith　「立刻地」。與 immediately 一樣，為口氣相當強硬的字眼，使用時須多加注意時機。◆ bill　「寄帳單給（某人），要求付款」。◆ Not only do I insist you immediately refund ～　「在要求您立即退款的同時，還～」。範例中的 not only ～ (but also) 的句型，因 I not only insist 中的副詞子句 not only 調到前面，而成為 do I 的倒裝句。而 I insist (that) you (should) immediately refund 的句子中，現在一般不加 should。

12-8 解約手續辦理完畢的通知

回函告知對方解約手續已辦理完畢，但因是在繳費截止日期的 7 天後，所以當月份也被要求付費。一併承諾對方將為其查詢退費事宜。

To: km234@mars.planet.co.jp
Subject: Re: Account Problems

Dear Kenji,

The account was closed on 8-30-97. That was 7 days after your billing cycle so that charge made it through. I will keep this mail and see if I can get the charge taken off.

Bobbie
feedback@birdnet.com

12-9 退款通知

承接上例（範例 12-8），通知退款的郵件。

To: km234@mars.planet.co.jp
Subject: Re: Account Problems

Dear Kenji,

I had the Billing Department refund the $9.95 charge, so you should see that on your next American Express bill.

Bobbie
feedback@birdnet.com

親愛的健司:

　　您的帳號已於 1997 年 8 月 30 日正式取消，但因那是在每月繳費截止日的 7 日後，故當月仍被要求付費。我將保留您的來函，並看看是否可以退還此筆帳款。

波比

【語句注釋】◆ 8–30–97 「1997 年 8 月 30 日」。如此類只用數字書寫日期的情況，在美國習慣用「日—月—年」。英國則習慣用「月—日—年」。因此為避免混淆，最好不要只以數字表示日期。在此範例中，因不可能有 30 月 8 日，故不會造成誤解。◆ billing cycle 「繳費週期」。例如，前一個月份的使用費，在隔月的 20 日繳納等的週期。◆ that charge made it through 「該筆請款照例通過」。that charge 是 made 的主詞。◆ see if ~ 「確認是否~」。◆ take off 「除去」。在此指取消付費。

親愛的健司:

　　我已請繳費部門退還 9 美元 95 美分的費用至您的美國運通卡下期帳單，敬請查對。

波比

【語句注釋】◆ had the Billing Department refund 「請繳費部門退款」。在此 have 為使役動詞，「have + 人 + 不加 to 的不定詞」，為「使某人（做）~」的意思。◆ you should see that ~ 「應該看到~」。在此 should 為「應該~」的意思。see 為「知道，看到」的意思。

在祝福對方女兒結婚的同時，一併傳達近況的一封信。

To: ykazuo@pc.web.or.jp
Subject: Re: Family News

Kazuo:

As you said, long time no see. Sorry for not responding earlier. I was doing a lot of running around and I was out of town for a while.

You wrote that your daughter got married on November 25. Congratulations are in order! Japanese wedding customs must be similar to the ones here, I guess? Don't worry about loneliness. When grandchildren enter the picture, you might find yourself really busy with them, as my father found out when my sister and her husband had their daughter. He loves every minute of it.

The job with Morris Management never worked out so I'll have to look for something else. The problem is I don't know what to look for anymore. Maybe it's because I did too many different things and now I need something really interesting. Something will eventually come up.

I'll try and make sure it doesn't take me much time to answer your mail again, so, hope to hear from you soon!

Regards,
Mandy

和夫：

　　如你所言，好久不見了。很抱歉沒能早點回信。最近可真是忙得團團轉，而且有一陣子我也出城去了。

　　你提到令嬡於 11 月 25 日結婚，在此獻上無限祝福。我猜日本婚禮的習俗也和這裏類似吧？別擔心會寂寞，將來孫子出世後，你可能會變得很忙碌哩！像我妹妹和妹婿生了女兒後，家父也有相同的感覺。他很喜歡與孫子共度每一分每一秒。

　　我在摩理斯經營管理公司的工作不太順利，所以必須另謀他職，問題是我已不知從何找起。或許是因為我前後做了太多不同的事情，而現在需要的是一個自己真正感到興趣的工作。我想我終會找到的。

　　我會儘早的回你的電子郵件，也希望很快能再聽到你的消息。

　　　　　　　　　　　　　　　　　　　　　　　　　　謹此
　　　　　　　　　　　　　　　　　　　　　　　　　　曼蒂

【語句注釋】◆ **long time no see** 「好久不見」。此為非正式的口語用法，表示通信雙方的交情深厚。注意不要使用於正式的書信中。◆ **a lot of running around** 「忙得團團轉」。run around 也可解釋為「到處走動」，但在此有「為許多事而忙碌」的感覺。◆ **in order** 「適切的，適當的」。例如在工作後，一般人會說 A beer is in order.（去喝杯啤酒吧！）。◆ **similar to the ones here** 「和這裏的情況（習慣）類似」。這裏的 ones 指的是 wedding customs。◆ **love every minute of it** 「非常的喜愛」。every minute of it 用於 love, enjoy, hate 等動詞之後時，有將動作的程度提至最高的作用。◆ **work out** 「（事情）進行得很順利，解決」。◆ **eventually** 「結局，到最後」。◆ **come up** 「（機會等）到來」。

傳送要求追加個人資料的傳真信函。

To: Mr. Henry Morgan
From: Rick Williams
Date: August 15
Number of pages (incl. cover): 1

Many thanks for your letter dated August 10.

We shall be happy to ship the items you require, but we need the following information before we can go ahead:

1. Your full name.
2. Your credit card expiry date.
3. Your credit card billing address (if different from the shipping address).

All the items on your order are in stock, and we will ship them as soon as you let us have the above information.

Yours sincerely,

收信人：亨利・摩根先生
發信人：瑞克・威廉斯
日期：8月15日
頁數（含書信開頭的第一頁）：全1頁

　　多謝您於8月10日的來信。
　　我們將很樂意地出口您所要求的商品，但在著手辦理各項手續之前，煩請您告知以下幾項資料：
　　1.您的全名。
　　2.信用卡的有效期限。
　　3.信用卡的付款地址（若與收貨地址不同時）。
　　您所訂購的各項商品都仍有庫存，在您告知上述資料後，我們將儘快出貨給您。

　　　　　　　　　　　　　　　　　　　　　　　　　　　　謹此

【語句注釋】◆ incl. cover 「包含書信開頭的第一頁」。指 including cover sheet。◆ dated ～ 「附有～日期」。dated 為舊式用法，現在也可用 of，如 your letter of August 10。◆ go ahead 「進行（計畫、工作等）」。◆ expiry 「期滿；有效期限」。亦作 expiration。◆ the items on your order 「您所訂購的項目」。這裏的 on 有「關於～」之意。◆ be in stock 「有庫存」。「缺貨」時則說 be out of stock。「庫存不足」則為 be short of stock。

透析商業英語的語法與語感

長野格 著

商業英語不只是F.O.B.等基本商業知識，潛藏在你我熟悉的字彙中的微妙語感與語法才是縱橫商場的不二法門，掌握了它，你將是名符其實的洽商高手。

- -

從身旁事物開始學習的 生活英語

古藤晃 著・本局編輯部 譯

每天食、衣、住、行所接觸到的事物，你知道如何用英語表達嗎？藉由學習身旁事物的英文用法，在實際生活中不斷運用，讓你從熟悉到活用，輕鬆掌握日常生活語彙。你老覺得周遭事物讓你有口難開嗎？你想加強你的生活英語會話嗎?那你千萬不可錯過本書！

國家圖書館出版品預行編目資料

社交英文書信 / Janusz Buda、長野格、城戶保男著;
　羅慧娟譯.－－初版二刷.－－臺北市；三民，民91
　面；　　公分
　譯自：Selected English letters for business people
　ISBN 957-14-3337-3　(平裝)

　1.英國語言-應用文　　2.商業書信

805.179　　　　　　　　　　　　　　　89017779

網路書店位址　http://www.sanmin.com.tw

© 社交英文書信

著作人　Janusz Buda　長野格　城戶保男
譯　者　羅慧娟
發行人　劉振強
著作財
產權人　三民書局股份有限公司
　　　　臺北市復興北路三八六號
發行所　三民書局股份有限公司
　　　　地址／臺北市復興北路三八六號
　　　　電話／二五○○六六○○
　　　　郵撥／○○○九九九八－－五號
印刷所　三民書局股份有限公司
門市部　復北店／臺北市復興北路三八六號
　　　　重南店／臺北市重慶南路一段六十一號
初版一刷　中華民國九十年一月
初版二刷　中華民國九十一年二月
編　　號　S 80365
基本定價　參元捌角
行政院新聞局登記證局版臺業字第○二○○號

有著作權‧不准侵害

ISBN　957-14-3337-3　(平裝)

林耀福等 主編 定價1500元

三民英漢大辭典

蒐羅字彙高達14萬字，片語數亦高達3萬6千。囊括各領域的新詞彙，為一部帶領您邁向廿一世紀的最佳工具書。

莊信正、楊榮華 主編 定價1000元

三民全球英漢辭典

全書詞條超過93,000項。釋義清晰明瞭，針對詞彙內涵作深入解析，是一本能有效提昇英語實力的好辭典。

三民廣解英漢辭典
謝國平 主編 定價1400元

收錄各種專門術語、時事用語達100,000字。例句豐富，並針對易錯文法、語法做深入淺出的解釋，是一部最符合英語學習者需求的辭典。

三民新英漢辭典
何萬順 主編 定價900元

收錄詞目增至67,500項。詳列原義、引申義，讓您確實掌握字義，加強活用能力。新增「搭配」欄，羅列慣用的詞語搭配用法，讓您輕鬆學習道地的英語。

三民新知英漢辭典
宋美璍、陳長房 主編
定價1000元

收錄中學、大專所需詞彙43,000字，總詞目多達60,000項。用來強調重要字彙多義性的「用法指引」，使讀者充份掌握主要用法及用例。是一本很生活、很實用的英漢辭典，讓您在生動、新穎的解說中快樂學習！

三民袖珍英漢辭典

謝國平、張寶燕 主編
定價280元

收錄詞條高達58,000字。從最新的專業術語、時事用詞到日常生活所需詞彙全數網羅。輕巧便利的口袋型設計，易於隨身攜帶。是一本專為需要經常查閱最新詞彙的您所設計的袖珍辭典。

三民簡明英漢辭典

宋美瑋、陳長房 主編
定價260元

收錄57,000字。口袋型設計，輕巧方便。常用字以＊特別標示，查閱更便捷。並附簡明英美地圖，是出國旅遊的良伴。

三民精解英漢辭典

何萬順 主編 定價500元

收錄詞條25,000字，以一般常用詞彙為主。以圖框針對句法結構、語法加以詳盡解說。全書雙色印刷，輔以豐富的漫畫式插圖，讓您在快樂的氣氛中學習。

謝國平 主編 定價350元

三民皇冠英漢辭典

明顯標示國中生必學的507個單字和最常犯的錯誤，說明詳盡，文字淺顯，是大學教授、中學老師一致肯定、推薦，最適合中學生和英語初學者使用的實用辭典！

莊信正、楊榮華 主編 定價580元

美國日常語辭典

自日常用品、飲食文化、文學、藝術、到常見俚語，本書廣泛收錄美國人生活各層面中經常使用的語彙，以求完整呈現美國真實面貌，讓您不只學好美語，更能進一步瞭解美國社會與文化。是一本能伴您暢遊美國的最佳工具書！

三民英漢辭典系列

Sanmin English-Chinese Dictionary

三民英語學習系列